MARRIAGE MADE
IN BLACKMAIL

MARRIAGE MADE IN BLACKMAIL

MICHELLE SMART

MILLS & BOON

First published in Great Britain 2018
by Mills & Boon, an imprint of HarperCollins*Publishers*
1 London Bridge Street, London, SE1 9GF

Large Print edition 2018

© 2018 Michelle Smart

ISBN: 978-0-263-07442-0

MIX
Paper from
responsible sources
FSC
www.fsc.org   FSC™ C007454

This book is produced from independently certified FSC™ paper to ensure responsible forest management. For more information visit www.harpercollins.co.uk/green.

Printed and bound in Great Britain
by CPI Group (UK) Ltd, Croydon, CR0 4YY

CHAPTER ONE

LUIS CASILLAS SNATCHED his ringing phone off the table and put it to his ear. *'Sí?'*

'Luis?'

'Sí.'

'It's Chloe.'

That brought him up short. 'Chloe… Chloe Guillem.'

The woman who had spent the past two months treating him as if he were a carrier for a deadly plague?

'Oui. I need your help. My car has broken down on a road on the Sierra de Guadarrama…'

'What are you doing there?'

'Driving. *Was* driving.'

'Have you called for recovery?'

'They can't get to me for two hours. My phone is running out of battery. Please, can you come and rescue me? Please? I don't feel safe.'

Luis looked at his watch and swore under his

breath. He was due at the gala he and his twin brother Javier were hosting in half an hour.

'Is there no one else you can call?' Chloe worked for his ballet company in Madrid. In the year the gregarious Frenchwoman had lived in his home city she had made plenty of friends.

'You are the closest. Please, Luis, come and get me.' Her voice dropped to a whisper. 'I'm scared.'

He took a long breath as he did some mental maths. This gala was incredibly important.

Ten years ago Luis and his twin had bought the provincial ballet company their prima ballerina mother had spent her childhood training at. Their aim had been to elevate it into a world-renowned, formidable ballet company. First they had renamed it Compania de Ballet de Casillas, in their mother's memory, then set about attracting the very best dancers and choreographers. Three years ago they had drawn up the plans to move the company out of the crumbling theatre it had called home for decades and into a purpose-built state-of-the art theatre with world-class training facilities and its own ballet school. Those plans had almost reached fruition.

Now they wanted patrons for it, members of the

elite to sponsor the ballet school and put it even more firmly on the world's ballet map. Europe's elite and dozens of its press were already gathering at the hotel. Luis *had* to be there.

'Where exactly are you?'

'You will come?'

It was the hope in her voice that did for him. Chloe had the sweetest voice he had ever had the pleasure of listening to. It wasn't girlishly sweet, more melodic, a voice that sang.

He couldn't leave her alone on the mountains.

'*Sí*, I will come and get you, but I need to know where you are.'

'I will send you the co-ordinates but then I will have to turn my phone off to save what is left of my battery.'

'Keep it on,' he ordered. 'Have you got anything to hand you can use as a weapon if you need it?'

'I'm not sure…'

'Find something heavy or sharp. Be vigilant. Send me the co-ordinates now. I'm on my way.'

'*Merci*, Luis. *Merci beaucoup.*'

'I'll be with you as soon as I can.'

Hurrying to his underground garage, he se-

lected the quickest of his fleet of cars, inputted
Chloe's co-ordinates into its satnav, then drove
it up the ramp. The moment he was clear, he
put his foot down, tearing down his long drive-
way, past the stretched Mercedes with his waiting driver in it.

His clever console, which had calculated the
quickest route for him, said he was an hour's
drive to her position from his home in the north
of Madrid, *if* he kept to the speed limit.

Provided traffic wasn't too heavy this Satur-
day evening, Luis estimated he could make it in
forty, possibly even thirty minutes.

He always kept to the speed limit in built-up
areas. The temptation to burn rubber was often
irresistible but he always controlled the impulse
until on the open road. Today, with thoughts of
Chloe stranded in the mountains on his mind, he
wove in and out of the traffic ignoring the blast
of horns hailing furiously in his wake.

Chloe Guillem. A funny, attention-seeking,
pretty child who had grown into a witty, fun-
loving, beautiful woman. Truly beautiful.

It had taken him a long time to notice it.

An old family friend, he hadn't seen her for

four or five years when she had called him out of the blue.

'*Bonjour*, Luis,' she had said in a sing-song tone that had immediately suggested familiarity. 'It is Chloe Guillem, little sister of your oldest friend, calling to ask you to put friendship ahead of business and give me a job.'

He had burst into laughter. After a short conversation where Chloe had explained that she'd completed her apprenticeship in the costume department of an English ballet company, spent the past two years working for a Parisian ballet company and was now seeking a fresh challenge, he'd given her the name and number of his Head of Costume. Recruitment, he'd explained, was nothing to do with him.

'But you own the company,' she had countered.

'I own it with my brother. We are experts in the construction business. We know nothing of ballet or how to make the costumes our dancers wear. That's what we employ people for.'

'I have references that say I'm very good,' she had cajoled.

'That is good because we only hire the best.'

'Will you put in a good word for me?'

'No, but if you mention that your mother was Clara Casillas's personal costume maker, I am sure that will work in your favour. Provided you are as good as your references say you are.'

'I am!'

'Then you will have no trouble convincing Maria to hire you,' he had laughed.

Luis had thought nothing more of the conversation until around six months later when he'd attended a directors meeting at the old theatre to discuss preparations for the company's move. A galloping gazelle had bounded up to him out of nowhere with a beaming smile and thrown her arms around him.

It had been Chloe, bright and joyous and, she had delightedly told him, loving her time in Madrid. Luis had been pleased to see this face from his past but he'd been too busy to take much notice of his old friend's little sister.

When Luis and Javier had pooled their meagre inheritance to form Casillas Ventures almost two decades ago, they had decided from the start that one of them would always be the 'point man' on each project. This would simplify matters for contractors and suppliers. Luis had taken the role of point man for the construction of the new theatre and facilities. In this venture he had been far more hands on than he would normally be but this was a special project. This was for their mother, a way for the world to see the Casillas name without automatically thinking of Clara Casillas's tragic end at the hands of her husband.

The closer it got to completion, the more hours he needed to put in, overseeing the construction and ensuring Compania de Ballet de Casillas was prepared for the wholesale move to its new premises.

From that embrace on though, whenever Luis visited the old crumbling theatre he somehow always managed to see Chloe.

She always acknowledged his presence, with either a quick wave if working on an intricate costume or a few words exchanged if on a break, her cheeks turning the colour of crimson whatever reception she gave, a little quirk he'd found intriguing but never given much thought to... not until he'd walked past a coffee shop a few months later and caught a glimpse of a raven haired beauty talking animatedly to a group of her peers. Spring had arrived in his home city and she'd been wearing a thin dress that exposed bare, milky-white arms, her thick raven hair loose and spilling over her shoulders.

He would have stopped and stared even if he hadn't recognised her.

How had he not seen it before?

Chloe Guillem *radiated*. Sunlight shone out of her pores, sexiness oozed from her skin. Her smile dazzled.

She must have felt his stare for she had looked up and seen him at the window and the full power of her smile had been unleashed on him and this time it had hit him straight in his loins. He had never in all his thirty-five years experienced a bolt of pure, undiluted, unfiltered lust as he had at that moment.

He'd taken her out to dinner that very night. It had been the most fun and invigorating evening he could remember. Chloe was funny, full of self-deprecating wit, a raucous laugh never far from her voluminous lips. And she was sexy.

Dios, was she sexy. He had been unable to tear his eyes away, greedily soaking up everything about her, all the glorious parts he'd been oblivious to. It was incredible to think he'd been blind to it for so long.

And the desire was mutual. Luis knew when a woman wanted him and Chloe's body language had needed little interpretation.

But when they had left the restaurant she had rebuffed his offer of a nightcap by hailing a taxi.

He had never been rejected before. It had intrigued rather than discouraged him.

'If not a nightcap how about a goodnight kiss?' he'd asked before she could escape into the cab, taking her face into his hands and gently rubbing his nose to hers. Her scent had filled his senses, reminding him of English strawberries and cream.

Her eyes had been stark on his, the flirtatious glimmer that had been prevalent the whole evening suddenly gone, her beautiful plump lips drawing together.

'Next time, *bonita*,' he had whispered, inhaling her scent again.

All the confusion on her face had broken into a smile that had shone straight into his chest. She had stepped back and nodded. 'Yes. Next time.'

'You will let me kiss you?'

The smile had widened, baby-blue eyes glittering with promise. 'Yes, I will let you kiss me.'

But there had been no next time and no kiss. Two days later everything had gone to hell with her brother. Chloe had cancelled their planned date and stopped accepting his calls. When he visited the ballet company she kept her head down and pretended not to see him.

They hadn't exchanged two words in almost as many months.

Why the hell he was tearing down roads at an average speed of a hundred miles an hour to rescue a woman who had dropped him like a hot brick he could not fathom, and especially on this night of all nights.

A curse flew from his lips when, thirty-four minutes after leaving his home, he reached the co-ordinates Chloe had given him.

It was a passing place on the winding road, with a flat grassy area for day-trippers to enjoy the spectacular view over a picnic. There was no one there. And no broken-down car.

He brought the car to a stop and grabbed his phone from the passenger seat. In his haste to get to her he'd forgotten to turn the ringtone up and only now did he see he had three missed calls from his brother.

He called Chloe. It went straight to voicemail.

Getting out of the car to search for her, he called Javier back.

'Where are you?' his brother snapped, picking up on the first ring.

'Don't ask. I'll be there as soon as I can.'

'I'm grounded in Florence.'

'What?' Javier was supposed to be at the gala already. In Madrid. Not Florence.

'My plane's been grounded on a technicality. It passed all the safety checks this morning. Not a single issue of concern. Something's not right.'

Luis disconnected the call, a real sense of disquiet racing through him. The sun was descending over Madrid in the far distance but the orange glow it emitted did nothing to stave off the chill that had settled in his bones.

His brother was grounded in Florence and suspected sabotage.

Luis had been lured to the middle of nowhere in the Sierra de Guadarrama in his dinner jacket, on a rescue mission where the damsel in distress had disappeared.

He checked the co-ordinates again.

This was definitely the right place.

So where the hell was she? And why was his sense of disquiet growing by the second?

Chloe Guillem took a seat in the first-class lounge at Madrid-Barajas airport and removed her phone from her carry-on bag.

She had six missed calls and seven text messages, all from the same number. She deleted the messages without reading them and fired off a message to her brother.

Mission accomplished. Waiting to board flight. x.

The glass of champagne she'd asked for when entering the lounge was brought to her table and she took a large sip of it at the moment her phone rang.

Cursing to herself, she switched it to silent and threw it down.

Two minutes later it vibrated in a dance over the table.

She had a new voicemail.

Her gut told her in the strongest possible terms not to listen to it.

She pressed play.

Luis Casillas's deep, playful voice echoed into her ear. 'Good evening, Chloe. I hope you are safe wherever you are and have not been kidnapped by a gang of marauding youths. You might wish you had been though because I *will* find you. And when I do...' Here, he chuckled malevolently. 'You will wish you had never crossed me. Sleep well, *bonita.*'

It was the emphasis on his final word rather than the implied threat that lifted the hairs on her arms.

Bonita.

The first time he had called her that she had thought she would never stop smiling.

Now she was overcome with the urge to cry.

He was not worth her tears, the two-faced, treacherous, conniving, evil bastard.

Thank goodness she'd had the sense to resist his offer of a nightcap...

Chloe downed the rest of her champagne and grimaced.

It hadn't been sense that had stopped her accepting his offer or his goodnight kiss. It had been fear.

Her date with Luis had given her a sense of joy she hadn't felt since her early childhood where she had spent innocent, happy days climbing trees and running around with friends, cocooned with love, blissfully unaware life could be anything other than wonderful. Luis was tied up in those memories.

Once upon a time she had been smitten with him.

She'd wanted to be sure his feelings for her were genuine and that he wasn't looking at her only as a potential conquest. As hard as it was, she'd wanted to trust him. She'd wanted his respect.

At the end of their date when his nose had rubbed against hers and every ounce of her being had strained on an invisible leash to escape her brain and *kiss* him, she had almost given in. She'd spent their entire date imagining him naked, something she'd blamed on the erotic dream she'd had of him the night before but which she'd known, deep down, was her own hidden sexuality breaking free for this man who'd stolen into her teenage heart and now demanded to be heard.

What had she been *thinking*?

Luis had no respect.

He had made a mockery of her brother's trust in him and by extension made a mockery of her and her dead mother. He was as bad, no, *worse*, than her pathetic father.

She knew his brother was equally culpable for ripping her brother off but Javier hadn't been the one to embrace her tightly at her mother's funeral and promise that one day the pain would get better. That had been Luis. Witty, sexy, fun-loving Luis, the only man who had ever captured her feminine attention. The only man in her twenty-five years she had ever dreamed of.

Whatever Benjamin had planned for him could not come soon enough.

The board on the wall with the constantly up-dated list of all departures and arrivals showed her own flight was now boarding.

Hurrying to her feet, Chloe made her way to the departure gate.

Now she knew what Luis Casillas was capable of she had to take his threat to hunt her down seriously.

Only when she looked out of the window of

her first-class seat on the flight paid for by her brother and watched Madrid shrink from view did her lungs loosen enough to breathe easily.

Luis thought he'd be able to find her? Well, good luck to him. She would be the needle to his haystack.

The Grand Bahaman suburb of Lucaya was, Chloe could not stop thinking, a paradise. Her brother had set her up in a villa in an exclusive complex where all her needs and whims were taken care of and all she had to worry about was keeping her sun lotion topped up.

She had spent her first six days there doing nothing but lazing by the swimming pool and refreshing her social media feeds, her worries slowly evaporating under the blazing sun. As far as boltholes went, this was the best. It had exclusivity but also, should Luis carry out his threat to hunt her down, the comfort of safety in numbers.

She doubted he was sparing her a moment of his thoughts. The fallout in Madrid and the rest of Europe was growing in intensity. Chloe read all the news and gossip torn between glee and heartbreak.

It should never have come to this. Luis and Javier should have done the right thing and paid her brother the money they owed him, all two hundred and twenty-five million euros of it.

Seven years ago, on the day Chloe and her brother were told their mother's cancer was terminal, Luis had called Benjamin for his help, dressing it up as an investment opportunity.

The Casillas brothers had paid a large deposit on some prime real-estate in Paris that they intended to build a skyscraper on that would eclipse all others. The owner of the land had suddenly demanded they pay the balance immediately or he would sell to another interested party. He'd given them until midnight. The Casillas brothers did not have the money. Benjamin did.

He gave them the cash, which amounted to twenty per cent of the total asking price. It was an eye-watering sum.

Tour Mont Blanc, as the skyscraper became known, took seven years to complete. Two months ago, Benjamin had received his copy of the final accounts. That was when he realised he'd been duped. The contract he'd signed, which he'd believed stated his profit share to be twenty per cent as had been verbally agreed between him and the Casillas brothers, had, unbeknown to him, been altered before he signed. He was entitled to only five per cent of the profit.

His oldest, closest friends had ripped him off. They'd taken advantage of him at his lowest point. They'd abused his trust.

When they'd refused to accept any wrongdoing Benjamin had taken them to court. Not only had he lost but the brothers had rubbed salt in the wound by hitting him with an injunction that forbade him from speaking out about any aspect of it.

Chloe would never have believed Luis could be so cold. Javier, absolutely, the man was colder than an ice sculpture, but Luis had always been warm.

Now the press was alive with speculation. Benjamin whisking Javier's prima ballerina fiancée away from the Casillas brothers' gala and marrying her days later had the rumour mill circling like an amphetamine-fed hamster on a wheel. An intrepid American journalist had discovered the existence of the injunction and now that injunction was backfiring. So far only the injunction itself was known about but a frenzy of speculation had broken out about the cause of it, none of it casting the Casillas brothers in a favourable light.

Let them be the ones to deal with it, Chloe thought defiantly, shoving her beach bag over her shoulder and slipping on her sparkly flip-flops. She was safe here in the Bahamas and her brother was safely cocooned with Freya in his chateau.

Leaving the tranquillity of the complex for only the third time since her arrival a week ago, she spent an enjoyable fifteen minutes strolling in the early-morning sun to Port Lucaya, very much looking forward to a day of island hopping on the complex owner's yacht.

The invitation had been hand delivered by the manager the evening before, the man explaining it was an excursion the owner provided for favoured guests whenever she visited. A guest had been taken ill so the invitation was Chloe's if she wanted it. Thinking she couldn't come to much harm if it was a woman hosting the event—she'd read too many horror stories about young women and rich men on yachts to have been comfortable with it being run by a rich male stranger—she had been delighted to accept. She couldn't spend a fortnight in the Bahamas hiding away.

Chloe liked to keep busy. She liked to be with people. Being alone with only her thoughts for company meant too much time to think. Better to let the past stay where it was by always looking forward and keeping her mind busy and her life full.

She found the port easily, the pristine yachts lined up in the small bay an excellent giveaway. Opposite it was the Port Lucaya Marketplace she'd heard so much about and which she had promised herself a visit to. Looking at the quaint colourful tourist trap bustling with life and exotic scents brought a big smile to her face. She would go there tomorrow.

Turning her attention back to the yachts, Chloe scanned them carefully, looking for the one named *Marietta*. Her excitement rose when she finally located it. At least four decks high, the *Marietta* was the biggest and most luxurious-looking of the lot. Not quite cruise-ship size, it looked big enough to accommodate dozens of guests with room to spare.

But where was everyone? The metal walkway

for passengers to board had been lowered but she saw and heard none of the sounds and sights you would expect of a large party going off on an all-inclusive day trip.

As she hesitated over whether to step onto the walkway, a figure wearing what she assumed was captain attire appeared on deck.

'Good morning,' he said, approaching her with a welcoming smile. 'Miss Guillem?'

She nodded.

'I am Captain Andrew Brand. Let me show you in. I'll give you the mandatory safety talk as we go.'

Chloe joined him on the gleaming yacht with a grin that only got wider as he showed off the magnificent vessel, pointing out the bar, swimming pool and hot tub on the next deck up, then taking her inside.

This yacht had *everything*, she thought in awe as she tried her hardest to pay attention to what she was being shown and told.

After showing her the Finnish sauna that had a window looking straight out to sea, he took her to the top deck to what was appropriately named 'the sky lounge' and left her with a young woman with tightly curled hair who made her a cock-tail of coconut blended with mango and rum and served it in the coconut shell with a straw. This stretched Chloe's smile so wide her mouth must have reached her ears. She enjoyed it so much she readily accepted a second, then took a seat on one of the plentiful cappuccino-coloured leather seats encircling the lounge.

She gazed out of one of the many windows, imagining the spectacular view of the stars at night from this wonderful vantage point, and hoped she would be lucky enough to experience it for herself. The estimated finish time of the day's excursion had been vague.

Which reminded her that she still seemed to be the only guest.

And where had the barwoman gone?

Unease crawling through her, Chloe opened her beach bag to search for her phone.

Just as her fingers closed on it, a tall figure stepped into the lounge.

Although the figure was only in the periphery of her vision, it was enough for her stomach to roil and ice to plunge into her veins.

Feeling very much like a teenager watching a

horror movie and wishing she could cover her eyes to hide from the scary bit, she slowly turned her head.

And there he stood, filling the space around him like a dark, menacing shadow, a grim smile on his face.

Luis.

'Hello, *bonita*. It is a pleasure to see you again.'

CHAPTER TWO

LUIS FELT IMMENSE satisfaction to read the horror in Chloe's baby-blue eyes.

'Nothing to say?' he taunted. 'I have travelled a long way to see you, *bonita*. I would have thought that deserved an enthusiastic welcome.'

Those wonderful pillowy lips he'd fantasised about kissing parted then snapped shut as she swallowed, shock clearly rendering her dumb.

'You're not normally this shy.' He folded his arms across his chest and stroked his jaw. 'Is it delight at seeing me that has struck you mute?'

Her wonderfully graceful throat moved, colour creeping over her cheeks. 'What…? How…?'

'Is that the best you can come up with?' He shook his head with mock incredulity.

She blinked rapidly and blew in and out. 'I've been set up.'

'The sun hasn't damaged your observation skills, I see.'

The baby-blue eyes stared straight into his. 'You bastard.'

'If we are moving straight to the name-calling, I have a select number of insults I can apply to you. Which shall I start with?'

'Forget it.' Hooking her large bag over her shoulder, she got to her feet. 'Let's not waste time. Say what you need to say. I have a holiday to enjoy.'

He gazed at the long legs now fully on display, only the top half of her supple thighs covered by the tight blue denim shorts she wore. *Dios*, for a She-Devil she had the most amazing body. Beauty, heavy breasts covered in a red T-shirt, a slim waist and a pert bottom…he defied any red-blooded heterosexual man out there not to fantasise about bedding her.

'My apologies,' he said sardonically. 'I didn't realise you were on a holiday. I thought you had run away.'

'No, it's definitely a holiday. Sun, sea, pina co-ladas and hot men.' She smiled as she listed the latter, a jibe he knew perfectly well was intended to cut at him. 'Getting far away from you was an added incentive but not the main consideration.'

'Would your brother have paid for you to holiday in the Bahamas if you hadn't agreed to do his dirty work?' The booking for her flights and villa had been paid for personally by Benjamin.

'Au contraire,' she said, switching from English to her native French. Between them they spoke each other's languages and English fluently. 'I didn't agree to do his dirty work. I insisted on it.' The smile she now cast him was pure beatific. 'Your gallantry at rescuing a damsel in distress does you credit. Knowing you were on those mountain roads searching for me is a thought I will cherish for ever.'

The rage that had simmered in his veins since he and Javier had pieced all the parts of the jigsaw together flashed through his skin.

Luis hadn't expected contrition from her but her triumph was something else.

Chloe had sent him on a wild goose chase so he would be late for the gala. Her brother had conspired to ground Javier's flight to Madrid so he too would be late for the gala. With both Casillas brothers out of the way and the world's media present, Benjamin had pounced, stealing Javier's fiancée away and taking her to his secure chateau in Provence. And then he had proceeded to black-mail them: Javier's fiancée in exchange for the money he claimed they owed him. If the money wasn't forthcoming he would marry her himself.

Luis could not remember the last time his brother had been so coldly furious. Javier had dug his heels in and refused to pay. For Javier it was a matter of principle. They had done nothing illegal and a court of law agreed with them. They didn't owe Benjamin a cent.

For Luis, Benjamin's actions were a declaration of war. All the guilt he'd felt and his plans to put things right between them had been discarded in an instant.

The press photographs of Freya leaving the gala hand in hand with Benjamin had captured a certain *something* between the pair of them that had made Luis wince for his brother. Whether Javier's fiancée was an unwitting tool in the plot or a willing supplicant was irrelevant. Those pictures had shown his brother's fiancée gazing into his enemy's eyes with a look of rapture on her face. Javier would rather starve than take her back.

His brother had been right not to take her back. Their enemy had married Freya two days ago, barely five days after stealing her away. The fall-out against the Casillas brothers had accelerated.

Chloe had willingly played her part in this. She would find herself playing a role to end it and whether that was willingly, he could not care less.

'Cherish those memories, *bonita*,' he said, hiding his anger with a beatific smile of his own. 'You earned them. You have proven yourself to be a fabulous actress.'

She fluttered her long black eyelashes at him. 'Were you worried about me? How touching.'

Remembering the burst of raw panic that had grabbed him to find her car missing from the place he had expected it to be… Worried, Luis concluded grimly, did not begin to cover it.

It was only because he had known her since she was in her mother's stomach, he told himself. For the first three years of Chloe's life he, Javier and Benjamin, all ten years older, had been her chief babysitters. None of them had been enthusiastic about the job, especially when she'd entered toddlerhood and turned into a pint-sized She-Devil.

More fool him for being so blown away by her adult beauty that he'd failed to see behind the fun-loving façade to the fully grown She-Devil beneath the milky skin.

'I would not be human if I hadn't been concerned,' he said blithely.

'I think it's debatable whether you and your brother are human at all.'

He spread his arms out and winked. 'Oh, I am *very* human, *bonita*, as I am more than happy for you to discover for yourself.'

A tinge of colour slashed her pretty rounded cheeks. She scowled at him and pulled her bag even closer into her side. 'Are we done yet? Have you finished with your fun?'

'Finished? *Bonita*, my fun with you has only just begun.'

Indeed, this was already much more fun than he had envisaged. Chloe's belligerent discomfort and outrage were things of beauty, acting like salve to his rabid anger.

'Yes, well, *my* fun is over. I'm going.'

'Going where?' he asked as she stomped to the door, giving him an extremely wide berth as she moved.

'Back to my villa.'

'How?'

It was the way he said that one word that made
Chloe pause and her heart accelerate even faster
and the sick feeling in her stomach swirl harder.

It didn't matter that Luis had found her, she
kept telling herself. It had been inevitable that
their paths would cross again one day. At least
it was done with and she could stop worrying
about it.

'Have you been so enraptured by my presence
that you failed to notice we're no longer at port?'
he mocked.

She turned her head to look out of the window
to her left. Then she turned it to the right.

Then she spun round to face the front, curses
flying through her head.

The captain had set the *Marietta* to sail and she
hadn't even noticed.

'Get this thing turned around right now!' she
demanded, eying him squarely.

He rubbed his chin. 'No, I don't think I will.'

'The captain will turn it round.' She took three
quick paces to the door and pressed the green
button beside it.

'That won't work,' he commented idly. 'The

crew have been instructed to leave us alone until further notice.'

'Take me back to port right now or I'm calling the police.'

He strode to the bar and laughed. It had a cruel, mocking tinge to it. 'Why ruin this wonderful reunion with talk of the police?'

She could have easily stamped her feet. 'Because you're holding me here against my will.'

He turned his back on her to study the rows of spirits, liqueurs and mixers lined up on the bar. 'Drink?'

'What?'

'I need a drink. Do you want one?'

'I want you to take me back to port. This game has gone on long enough.'

'This is no game, *bonita*.'

'Stop *calling* me that.'

He looked at her and winked. 'I remember when it made you blush.'

'That was before I knew what kind of a man you really are, you unscrupulous jerk. And stop winking at me. If this isn't a game, stop acting like it is.'

'If I am acting like it's a game, you conniving

witch, it's to stop myself from grabbing you by the shoulders and shaking you until your teeth fall out.' He flashed his perfectly white and perfectly straight teeth at her. 'Or from taking the kiss you owe me.'

She sucked in a sharp breath.

His threat didn't bother her because she instinctively knew Luis would never lay a finger on her in anger.

But the mention of the kiss she owed him...

Chloe spent her days surrounded by dancers. The male ones had the most amazing physiques and they worked hard to maintain them, the look they strove for lean and strong. To her eyes they were beautiful sculptures but not sexy.

Luis was a hulk of a man, burly and rugged, a man for whom chest waxing would be considered a joke. If he had any vanity she'd never seen it. Even his dark hair, which he kept long on top and flopped either side of his forehead, never looked as if he did more to it than run his fingers through it when he remembered.

Square jawed, his hazel eyes surrounded with laughter lines, his nose broad, cheekbones high, lips full but firm, the outbreak of stubble never far beneath his skin.

In a world of metrosexual men, Luis was a man who drank testosterone for breakfast and made no apologies for it. He would be as comfortable chopping wood with an axe as he would holding a meeting in a boardroom and she found him *very* sexy.

She'd dreamed of kissing him when she was seventeen years old, dreams that had faded to a hazy memory over the years but then re-awoken with a vengeance when she had started work at Compania de Ballet de Casillas. Months after she'd joined the company Luis had turned up. She had been delighted to see him, had spontaneously thrown her arms around him and been completely unprepared for the surge of heat that had bathed her upon finding herself pressed against his hard bulk in that fleeting moment.

That heated feeling had been with her ever since. All she'd needed was one glimpse of him and her heart would pound. She would smile and try to act nonchalant but had been painfully aware of her face resembling a tomato.

That heat was there now too, vibrating inside

her. Not even the knowledge of his treachery had dimmed it. She hated herself for that.

He looked up from the bottle of black vodka he was examining and smiled unpleasantly. 'The insults hurt, don't they?'

'You deserve yours and more for what you did to my brother.' And to me, she refrained from adding.

Learning how deeply he'd betrayed her brother had cut her like a knife. The more she and Benjamin had put the pieces together, the deeper the cut had gone, all the way back to her earliest memories.

Had Luis and Javier always had contempt for her family? Or had the damage done by their mother's horrific murder at the hands of their father been the root cause of it?

Their mothers had been closer than sisters. As far back as Chloe could remember Luis and Javier had been a part of their lives. They would come and stay with them for weeks at a time in the school holidays then, when she had reached eight and them eighteen and they had snubbed university to set out on their own path, they would still drop in for visits whenever they were in Paris.

Their visits had always made her mother so happy. When she'd been diagnosed with lung cancer they had been there for all of them. Luis had visited her mother so many times in hospital the staff had assumed he was one of her children.

Had the supposed feelings he'd had for her family all been a lie? If not, then how could he have tricked her brother into signing that contract on the day their mother's condition was diagnosed as terminal?

Luis replaced the bottle of vodka in his hand with a bottle of rum, twisted the cap off and sniffed it. 'Whatever we did to your brother he has repaid with fire. He has gone too far and so have you. Thanks to you and your brother conspiring against me and *my* brother, our names are mud.'

'Good. You deserve it.' She hated the quiver in her voice. Hated that being so close to him evoked all those awful feelings again that should never have sprung to life in the first place.

Her heart shouldn't beat so wildly for this man. She swallowed before adding, 'You took advantage of him when our mother was dying. I hope the journalist investigating the injunction unveils your treachery to the world and that everyone learns what lying, cheating scumbags the Casillas brothers are.'

Hazel eyes suddenly snapped onto hers, a nitrogen-cold stare that sent a snake of ice coiling up her spine. 'We did not cheat your brother.'

'Yes, you did. I don't care what that court said. You ripped him off and you know it.'

His nostrils flared before he stretched out a hand to the row of cocktail mixers. 'I am going to tell you something, *bonita*. I had sympathy for Benjamin's position.'

'Of course you did,' she scorned with a shake of her hair.

'The terms of profit were reduced from twenty per cent to five per cent under the advice of our lawyer. Your brother's contribution to the project was a portion of the funding whereas Javier and I would be doing all the work.'

Luis remembered that conversation well. It was one of only a few clear recollections from a day that had flown by at warp speed as he and Javier had battled to salvage the deal they had put so much time and money into.

'You agreed on twenty per cent. That was a verbal agreement.'

He added crushed ice to the concoction he'd put in the cocktail shaker. 'Benjamin was sent a copy of the contract to read five hours before we all signed it. He didn't read it.'

Javier had been the point man on the Tour Mont Blanc project and emailed the contract to Benjamin. Luis had been unaware of his twin's failure to mention the change in the profit terms in that email. When they had gone to his apartment to sign it, the atmosphere had been heavy, the news of Benjamin's mother overshadowing everything.

Luis had only discovered three months later, at Louise Guillem's funeral of all days, that Benjamin still thought he would be receiving twenty per cent of the profit. It had been a passing comment during the wake, Benjamin nursing a bottle of Scotch and staring out of his chateau's window saying he didn't know how long he would have to keep the wolves from the door and ruefully adding that, if only the Tour Mont Blanc project could be speeded up and he had his twenty per cent profit now, all his money troubles would be over.

Luis had had many arguments with his brother through the years but that had been the closest they had ever come to physical blows. Javier had been immovable: Benjamin should have read the contract.

His twin was completely hard-nosed when it came to business. Luis was generally hard-hearted when it came to business too. They weren't running a charity, they were in the business of making money and at the time their bank balance had been perilously close to zero.

But Benjamin had been their oldest friend and Luis had been very much aware that Benjamin's frame of mind on the day of the signing had been anywhere but on the contract.

With Javier digging his heels in, Luis had decided that it would only cause bad feeling and acrimony if he told Benjamin the truth. It had been better for everyone that Luis wait for Tour Mont Blanc, a project that would take years, to be completed and for all the money to be in the bank before speaking to Benjamin man-to-man about it and forging a private agreement on the matter.

'He didn't read it because he was cut up about our mother. He *trusted* you. He had no idea the terms had been changed. He signed that contract in good faith.' Chloe's eyes were fixed on his, ringed with loathing. 'He gave you the last of his cash savings. That investment meant he couldn't afford to buy the chateau outright and he had to get a huge mortgage to pay for it so our mother could end her days there. He almost lost everything in the aftermath. You took his money then watched him struggle to stop himself from drowning.'

'We were not in a position to help him. It gives me no pleasure to admit this but we were in as dire a financial situation as Benjamin was. We'd grown too big too soon and over-extended massively. The difference between us and Benjamin was that Benjamin saw no shame in admitting it. We did, and I am only sharing this with you so you understand that I'm not the treacherous bastard you think I am. At that time we were *all* trying to save ourselves from drowning. I'd always had it in the back of my mind that when the

Tour Mont Blanc project was complete I would come to a private agreement with Benjamin and pay him the extra profit he felt he was due...'

'You didn't do that though, did you? The first he knew of it was when he saw the final accounts!'

'I'd been overseeing a project in Brazil. Javier sent the accounts before I had the chance to talk to Benjamin about it. I flew back for Javier's engagement party and your brother came in all guns blazing firing libellous accusations at us. Call it human nature, call it bull-headedness but when someone threatens me my instinct is to fight back. I admit, ugly words were exchanged that day—we were all on the defensive, all of us, your brother included. He would not discuss things reasonably...'

'Why should he have?' She stared at him like a beautiful, proudly defiant elfin princess, arms folded belligerently across her ample chest, as sexy a creature as could be imagined.

Luis still struggled to comprehend how he'd been oblivious to her beauty for all those months or how he could be standing there with the woman who had conspired against him and his twin and find his blood still pumping wildly for her. He didn't know which need he wanted to satisfy the most: the need to avenge himself or the need to throw her onto the nearest soft furnishing and take that delectable body as his own.

Soon he would do both. He would screw her over in more ways than one.

'Humans respond better to reason. Fight or flight, *bonita*. Benjamin made threats, we dug our heels in, then he hit us with the lawsuit and we had no choice but to defend ourselves. But I still had sympathy for his position. In truth it is something that hadn't sat well with me for many years. I'd hoped to speak to him privately and come to an agreement once the litigation was over with and tempers had cooled and we could speak as rational men. Legally, I had nothing to prove. Javier and I had done nothing wrong and that's been vindicated in a court of law.'

'If you really believed that, why take the injunction out on him?'

'Because there has been enough rubbish in the past two decades about my family. Do you have any idea how hard it is being Yuri Abramova and Clara Casillas's sons?' Luis downed his cocktail and grimaced at the bitter taste that perfectly matched his mood.

He tipped the glass he'd filled for Chloe down the bar's sink and reached for a fresh cocktail shaker.

'We are the sons of a famous wife killer,' he continued as he set about making a more palatable cocktail, one that would hopefully wash away the bile lodged in his throat. 'It is one of the most infamous murders in the past century. There have been documentaries made about it, books and endless newspaper articles. A Hollywood studio wanted to make a movie about it. Can you imagine that? They wanted to turn my mother's death at the hands of my father into entertainment.'

Chloe tried her hardest not to allow sympathy to creep through her but it was hard. Luis's past was something that never failed to make her heart twist and tears burn her eyes. She blinked them back now as she imagined the vulnerable thirteen-year-old he would have been.

She had been only three when Luis's mother had been murdered, far too young to have any memories of it.

But she *had* been there.

Clara had been performing in London on the night of her murder in a production of *Romeo & Juliet*. Yuri, a ballet dancer who had defected from the old USSR in the seventies and whose career had gone into freefall, had watched the performance convinced his wife was having a real-life affair with Romeo. When the performance had ended, Yuri had locked Clara in her dressing room, preventing dancers and backstage staff from entering when the screams and shouts had first rung out.

By the time they'd smashed the door open, Clara was dead, Yuri's hands still around her throat.

Luis and Javier had been in the hotel across the road from the theatre babysitting Chloe with Benjamin.

Chloe and Benjamin's mother, Louise, who had loved the twins fiercely, had been the one to break the terrible news to them.

He poured the fresh cocktail into two clean glasses. 'Imagine what it has been like for us growing up with that as our marker. We are hugely successful and rich beyond our wildest dreams but still people look at us and their first thought is our parents. You see it in their eyes, curiosity and fear.'

He pushed one of the glasses towards her and put the other to his lips. He took a sip and pulled a musing face. 'Not too bad. Better than the last one but I think I'll stick to construction and property developing.' He took another sip. 'As I was saying. My parents. A legacy we have tried hard to escape from while still honouring our mother.'

'Is that why you took her surname?' The question came before she could hold it back. It was something she'd been intensely curious about for years.

'We took it because neither of us could endure living with our father's name. We have worked hard to disassociate ourselves from that man and to make our mother's name synonymous with the beauty of her dance and not the horror of her death, but now everything has been dredged up again and *you* are partly responsible. Our lives are back under the media's lens and again we find the world wondering how much of our father's murderous blood lives in our veins.' He inhaled deeply. 'We took out the injunction to stop this very thing from happening because we knew Benjamin was an explosive primed to detonate. We are close to signing a deal to build a new shopping complex in Canada. Our partner in this venture has stopped returning our calls.'

'Then he's a smart man who knows he will be ripped off.'

The flash of anger that rippled from Luis's eyes was enough to make her quail.

'We did *not* rip him off and if anyone says otherwise we will sue the clothes off their back.'

'You ripped my brother off,' she said defiantly. 'Feel free to sue me. I would love my day in court.'

'I have a much better way of dealing with *you*, *bonita*, but as for your brother, I will not say this again—we did not rip him off. I was going to get the gala out of the way and then call him but, instead, Benjamin stole Freya and tried to blackmail us. All my sympathy left me then. As far as I'm concerned, your brother can go to hell. The press speculation his actions have wrought are untenable. My assistant found comments on a newspaper website querying whether Freya ran off with Benjamin because she feared she would end up like my mother.'

Chloe winced. She had many issues with Luis and Javier but they could no more help their parentage than she could help hers. 'That's disgusting.'

'I'm glad you think so because you are going to help put things right. If you hadn't called with your tale of terror I would have been at the gala before Benjamin stepped foot inside it. None of this would have happened.'

'He believed you owed him two hundred and twenty-five million euros,' she spat, her fleeting compassion overridden by anger. 'Did you expect him to roll over and accept that? Did you expect *me* to? I was there with him at the hospital when you made that call begging for his help and his money.'

She'd been there, at the first turn of the wheel of the whole mess.

Chloe had been sitting on a bench in the hospital garden with her big brother, both of them dazed; her crying, he ashen, both struggling to comprehend the mother they loved so much was going to die. That was when Benjamin had received the call from Luis asking for his financial help.

'If you felt Javier had been cheated would you sit there meekly and allow it to go unchallenged when there was something practical you could do to help?'

'Probably not.' He shrugged. 'But would I have conspired to kidnap a woman and hold her to ransom…? No, I would not have gone that far if the first throw of the dice had not already been rolled.'

'I did not conspire to kidnap Freya! I helped whisk her away from a potential marriage made in hell and…'

'Is that how you justify it to yourself? I must remember to dress my actions up in a similar fashion when I tell you that you won't be returning to port until you have married me.'

CHAPTER THREE

FOR A MOMENT there was an intense buzzing in Chloe's ears. She shook her head to clear it, being careful not to take her eyes from Luis, who was now leaning forward with his elbows on the bar.

'What are you talking about?'

His eyes were intense on hers. 'I've not kidnapped you, I've borrowed you. Would that be how it's said? Is that how I can justify it?'

'No, what was that rubbish about marrying me?'

'That? That's the next stage. If you want to go home you have to marry me first. But let us not call it blackmail. By your logic it will be…an incentive? How does that sound?'

'It sounds like your cocktail has gone straight to your head.'

'And you haven't drunk yours yet. Try it. You might surprise yourself—and me—and like it.'

'Not if it makes me as drunk as *you* clearly are.'

'Regretfully, I am not drunk but I *am* serious.'

The hairs on her arms lifted, coldness creeping up her spine and into her veins. She hugged her bag closer to her. 'Okay, this game stops now. I'm sorry for my part in the affair. Is that what you want to hear? Okay then, how about this? I was wrong, I apologise. I'm sorry...*je suis desolée... lo siento...mi dispiace...*'

Amusement flickered in his hazel eyes. 'Can you apologise in Chinese too?'

'If that's what you want I'll teach myself it and say it to you, just *let me go.*'

The spacious windowed walls of the lounge were closing in on her. Suddenly it felt imperative to get off this yacht. She needed dry land and space to run as far and as fast as she could. Luis's defence of himself, his hulking presence, his magnetism...it was all too much.

It had always been too much but it had never scared her before, not like this.

She had such awareness for this man. She remembered all the visits he'd made to the theatre when she'd been working there, how she would sense his presence in the building long before she caught sight of him, almost as if she had an internal antenna tuned to his frequency. That antenna was as alert now as it had ever been and vibrating like the motor of a seismograph recording an earthquake.

She needed to find safety before the ground opened up and swallowed her whole.

He studied her silently, the brief amusement disappearing into seriousness. 'I warned you in my message that I would find you and that you would live to regret crossing me,' he told her slowly. 'You have known me long enough to know I am not a man to make idle threats.'

'Believe me, right now I am regretting it.'

'You're only regretting that I found you, not your actions.'

She opened her mouth to lie and deny it. His denials about not being party to Benjamin signing the contract under false pretences and that he'd wanted to put things right had sounded so sincere that there had been a few moments when she'd wondered if he might be speaking the truth.

His threats to marry her made her glad she hadn't swallowed those lies.

It would never happen. *He* could go to hell first.

Hell was where he belonged, him and his cold monster of a brother.

'I can see the truth in your eyes, *bonita*,' Luis said grimly before she could speak. 'You don't believe me and you don't regret your actions. In many respects I commend you for your loyalty to your brother.'

It was a loyalty he understood.

Luis and Javier had always been loyal to each other. Though far removed from the other in looks and personality, they had grown and developed in the same womb and the bond that bound them together was unbreakable, tightened by the tragedy of their lives.

'Benjamin's own sister marrying me will kill the rumours and stop people believing that Javier and I are the devil's spawn. It's the only way to repair the damage.'

'I would rather swim to shore than marry you,' she spat, not caring at that moment that she'd never even mastered a basic doggy paddle.

'It will be the only way you get home if you don't agree to it.' He placed his chin on his knuckles. 'But have no worries, *bonita*. I am happy to wait for as long as is needed for you to come to the correct decision.'

'Then we will sail these seas for ever because I will never, ever, marry you and there is nothing you can do to make me.' She smiled tremulously. 'You can't threaten to fire me—I've already quit.'

It didn't escape his attention that she was inching her way to the door. Any moment she would bolt on those long gazelle-like legs.

Let her run. Chloe would soon discover there was no escape.

He returned the smile. 'You have not worked your notice period. I can sue you for that and I can sue you for breach of contract.'

'What have I breached?'

'You passed on confidential information about one of our dancers to your brother.'

'Freya's not an asset, she's a person.'

'She's a company asset. You acted as a spy against our interests.'

'You would have to prove it. Look at their wedding photo. It's obvious they're in love with each other.' Her beautiful smile widened but there was a growing wildness in her eyes. 'See? My instincts were right. Benjamin took her to punish

Javier but he already wanted her for himself and she wanted him. You can sue me for whatever you want but if you won it wouldn't matter; Benjamin would pay any fine.'

'I could make sure you never work in the ballet world again.'

'I'm sure you could and without much effort but I don't care. I survived on an apprentice's salary, I'll cope. I don't care what job I do. I'll wait tables or clean bathrooms.'

'You would throw your career away?'

Her heart-shaped chin lifted. 'Some things are more important. I knew the risk I was taking when I made the call to you.'

'Interesting,' he mused. 'You will be pleased to know I have no wish to destroy you. Your brother? *Sí.* I would gladly destroy him but the feud can end here and now—call it an additional incentive. All you have to do is marry me and all the bad blood will be over.'

'You call that an incentive?' she said disdainfully. 'There is nothing more you can do to hurt him than you have already done.'

'Any hurt caused was not deliberate,' he asserted through gritted teeth.

'You would say that. You wanted me to feel guilty enough that I agreed to your nefarious plan. Well, it hasn't worked. I don't believe you ever intended to give him any of the profit you denied him and I regret nothing. I will never marry you.'

The last of Luis's patience snapped.

He'd only been prepared to make up the profit shortfall because Benjamin was his oldest friend. In truth, despite his bulging contact book, Benjamin was his only real friend.

But Benjamin had not just crossed a line, he'd hacked at it with a chainsaw and the damage caused by his actions had the potential to destroy both Casillas brothers. Reputations could be broken by the smallest means and businesses ruined. Luis had not been exaggerating when he'd spoken of the financial troubles he and Javier had got into seven years ago. There had been an eighteen-month period when they had struggled to find the cash to put petrol in their cars but then three projects were completed within months of each other and suddenly the money had started rolling in. Almost a decade of complete focus and hard work and suddenly they were richer than they had ever dreamed possible. Their fortune had only grown since.

He would not be poor again. He would not have his or his brother's reputation battered any more. Chloe could put a stop to all of it with two simple words: I do.

'I have explained the facts of the situation,' he said tightly. 'If you choose not to believe them then so be it but this ends now. Too much damage has been caused. Marry me and no one else need be hurt.'

'Apart from me.'

'How will marriage hurt you? You're a single woman—'

'We went on one date two months ago,' she interrupted hotly. 'You've no idea who I've seen since then.'

He mustered a smile. 'You said only an hour ago that you were on a holiday that involved hot men. That implies you are either single or a cheat. Which is it?'

Her cheeks had turned red enough to warm his hands on them. 'I'm a grown woman. How I conduct my personal life is my business.'

He shrugged. 'Lover or not, you're an unmarried woman. Your career is in tatters… What will you be giving up to marry me and rectify the mess you helped create? It wouldn't be a permanent marriage, only one that lasts long enough to shut the wolves up and restore my and my brother's reputations. In return, I would give you everything your heart desires.'

'My heart does not desire *you.*'

'Your body does.' At the outraged widening of her eyes, his smile broadened. 'I do not forget the kiss you owe me or the way your hungry eyes looked at me.'

Somehow her cheeks managed to turn a shade darker but she tossed her hair over her shoulders defiantly. 'That was the wine talking.'

His laugh at her barefaced lie was genuine. Even now, with all the acrimony and anger between them, that undercurrent remained, thick enough to taste. 'Do you want to prove that?'

'I don't have to prove anything. I don't want to marry anyone, not even for a short time, and if I did you would be the last man on the list. I won't do it. Promise what you want, make all the threats you like, I'm not going to marry you. The end.' Her hand grabbed the handle of the door that led outside. 'This isn't the Middle Ages. Women are not chattels to be bought or traded. As fun as this conversation has been, I'm going.'

Turning her back to him, Chloe stepped out onto the deck. After the air conditioning of the sky lounge it was like stepping into a furnace, the sun high above them and beaming its rays onto her skin.

She would find a way off this yacht even if she had to row her way back to shore. She'd just have to wear a life-jacket.

All she could see to the horizon was the Caribbean Sea, shining brilliantly blue under the azure sky.

She shivered to think what creatures lay beneath the still surface.

She spotted the stairs that led to the deck below and hurried down them.

'Where are you going to go?'

Heart pounding, she paused to look up.

Luis's arms were hanging over the balustrade at the top of the stairs, his handsome, sexy face smirking down on her but that hardness still glinting in his eyes.

'I'm going to find the captain and tell him to

take us back to shore,' she told him with all the defiance in her veins.

'I bought the *Marietta* from her namesake three days ago. The captain answers to me.'

'But the manager said it belonged to the owner...'

'I bribed him,' he said matter-of-factly, without an ounce of shame. 'Marietta doesn't own the complex in Lucaya.'

She stared up at him as she processed what he'd said. 'You bought a yacht to trap me on?'

'I have often considered the idea of a yacht and now I have one.'

'Just like that?'

'I had a spare two hundred million sitting in a bank account. I was going to use that money to settle with your brother...that money enabled me to make Marietta an offer she couldn't refuse.'

Her stomach cramped to imagine what other factors he had brought to the negotiating table with Marietta. If his reputation was anything to go by it was more likely to have been a negotiating bed.

Wherever he'd done his negotiations for it, knowing he'd bought this yacht with the primary purpose of trapping her almost had her struck dumb.

Seven years ago it would have thrilled her.

From the age of seventeen she'd developed an intricate fantasy in her head where Luis waited for her to become a fully mature woman then declared his undying love for her and whisked her down the aisle.

That memory, not thought of in years, lanced her.

Once upon a time she had dreamed of marrying *him*.

How idyllic she had been. And how starved for affection.

She'd woven the fantasy while living under her father's roof for the first time in her life, mourning the mother she had loved with all her heart and coping with her remaining parent's indifference. His indifference shouldn't have hurt, not after a life spent where he'd been nothing but a name, but he was her *father*. His blood ran in her veins. They shared the same nose and ears.

Once she had moved out of that awful, unloving home the fantasies about Luis had petered away. She'd had a career to embark on and she'd been determined to put the past behind her and get out there and live her life to the fullest.

It had been the biggest shock to her system to re-enter Luis's orbit and discover her old craving for him hadn't withered into nothing, just been pushed into dormancy.

It felt like poison in her veins to imagine the debauched parties he would host on this beautiful yacht.

He moved from the balustrade and put his hand on the rail as he made the slow walk down the steps. That dangerous glint remained in his eyes but there was amusement within the hazel swirl too. 'Have you not yet realised I am a man who plans everything down to the last detail?'

Her throat closed at his approach. She stepped back, off the bottom step and onto the safety of the deck.

His smile grew with every step he took closer to her. 'Your brother is good with details too. I have thought about how he was able to steal Freya and keep her under lock and key. Seclusion with only trusted employees was how he achieved it. He even got her to marry him, the clever man. I thought if such a ploy is good enough for Benjamin then it is good enough for me. All I had to do was work the details. The yacht is mine and the crew are in my employ. They obey orders directly from me and I am paying them enough to ensure their loyalty.'

She took another step back. 'Not everyone's loyalty can be bought. And don't come any closer.'

The faint amusement that had lurked in his eyes faded away as he came to a stop barely two feet from her.

For a long moment neither of them spoke. Chloe, trapped in the sudden intensity of his stare, felt her heart clench into a fist then burst into an erratic beat that echoed up her throat.

Then a tight smile formed on those sensual lips and he spread his arms out. 'Search wherever you like. Speak to whoever you like. When you are satisfied you have nowhere to escape, come and find me.'

And then he walked back up the steps, leaving her standing there, her nails digging into the palms of her hands.

She would find a way off this yacht. She would. And then she would bring the full force of the law down on him.

* * *

Luis disconnected the call from his brother and bowed his head to dig his fingers through his hair, doing his best to rub the forming headache out of his skull.

He had finally got hold of George, their Canadian partner in their venture to build the largest shopping complex in the northern hemisphere. George was one of the richest and most powerful men in North America. After much coaxing, he had agreed to a video conference. However, he had insisted it be held in the morning.

Just as they had suspected, George was seriously considering pulling out of the agreement. Without George as their partner, the permits needed would be revoked.

Unfortunately he'd insisted Javier be in attendance for the call too.

Luis swore as he thought of his brother's foul mood. His brother was like a stick of old highly temperamental dynamite ready to explode at the slightest provocation.

Even if he succeeded in getting Javier to put on a human front, Luis knew it would not be enough. Their Canadian partner was an old-school tycoon who believed in a man's word being his bond. It was the injunction he and Javier had taken out against Benjamin that would be the biggest hurdle to overcome.

That damn injunction. At the time, with Benjamin then the one behaving like a stick of temperamental dynamite, it had seemed necessary. They had rushed it through, knowing time was of the essence. Now it only served to make them look guilty over a matter in which they had broken no law.

If George pulled out of the project, the consequences were unimaginable. It wasn't the money, it was what it represented. If he pulled out he was essentially telling the world that the Casillas brothers were not men who could be trusted to do business with. It would prove fatal to their already battered reputations.

With Chloe as Luis's wife, all of George's doubts would be allayed and the dominoes would stop falling but until he got his ring on her finger he would have to play for time.

He'd known from the first look at the pictures of Freya and Benjamin leaving the gala hand in hand how the situation would be played out in the media. He and his brother would be painted as the devils. Their parents' history would be dredged up and played to fit the media's narrative of them. The idea of marrying Chloe had floated into his mind almost immediately bringing with it a flicker of excitement through his loins. Punishment and vindication all in one neat move.

Chloe had become an itch he could not purge in more ways than one, a taunt in his dreams, and suddenly he'd been presented with the motives to scratch it all away.

He'd known her well enough to know she wouldn't agree to marriage without a fight. Chloe had been born stubborn...

The door from the deck suddenly flew open and she burst into the lounge, raven hair spraying in all directions.

In one skip of a heart his burgeoning headache and weariness disappeared and his mood lifted.

He straightened in his chair, taking in everything about her afresh.

She glared at him, her chest heaving as she struggled for breath.

Then those wonderful voluptuous lips parted. 'I *hate* you.'

CHAPTER FOUR

TWO WHOLE HOURS Chloe had wasted going from room to room, speaking with crew member after crew member, her panic growing with each brief conversation. Surely her pleas for help would be met with sympathy from *someone*? Instead she had gained the distinct impression they didn't understand what she was complaining about.

Either that or they were used to histrionics. They probably assumed she was some spoilt rich girl who'd had a fight with her boyfriend.

The worst of it was that Chloe had always prided herself on *never* having histrionics. Only once had she succumbed to it and it had ended with her moving out of her father's house and moving in with her brother. She hadn't spoken to her father since that awful argument.

Luis sat casually on a chair with his elbows resting on his thighs, his hazel eyes fixed on her with what looked like calm amusement that raised her blood pressure to critical levels.

How could he be so calm when her entire life was being pulled out from beneath her?

'When I get away I am going to make it my mission in life to destroy you.'

'I'm terrified.' He stretched his back. 'I assume you didn't find an escape route?'

How badly she hated him, his arrogance, his cruelty, his entitlement.

And how badly she despised herself for having a heart that still jolted violently just to look at him.

Why were these awful emotions for this man still inside her, after everything he had done? She could forgive her just-turned-seventeen-years-old self for blithely overlooking his reputation as a ladies' man in the dreams she had created about him but she was an adult now, with adult thoughts and responses.

She could not forgive herself for it still being him, with all his treachery and lies, evoking so *much* inside her.

'How much are you paying the crew to turn a

blind eye? It must be a fortune. Not one of them is prepared to help me.'

'I hope they refused politely.'

'They are incredibly well trained and polite.'

'Good.' He smiled with satisfaction. 'Marietta assured me they were the most loyal crew on the seas.'

For some reason the name Marietta only enraged her further.

She didn't want to think about the negotiations that had taken place for Luis to take ownership of this floating prison in such super-quick time. It made her feel as if she had ants crawling all over her skin.

'Now you are back we can have something to eat.'

Chloe breathed heavily, trying her hardest to keep some semblance of control when all she wanted to do was kick and punch him into reason. She had known there was a risk in crossing Luis but she had never dreamed he would go to these lengths.

She had no means of escape until they reached land.

'I'm not hungry.'

'Yes you are. How can you hope to escape if you're faint with hunger?'

'How can you be so blasé?' she demanded angrily. 'You have *kidnapped* me.'

'Borrowed,' he corrected as his phone suddenly rang. He stretched an arm out to pick it up.

His infuriating arrogance, already burrowing under her skin like a pulse, pushed her over the edge, all her fears and panic peaking.

She could contain it no more.

Chloe charged at him, snatched the phone from his hand before he could speak into it and threw it onto the floor as hard as she could. Only two humongous arms wrapping around her waist and yanking her backwards into a solid wall of man stopped her from stamping on it.

'Let me go,' she screamed, struggling against the vice-like hold she'd been put in, but it was like fighting against a solid strait-jacket.

His hold around her tightened and then she was lifted off her feet and placed unceremoniously onto a sofa. She hardly had time to catch a breath before her arms were pinioned above her head, her wrists secured together with one of his hands and Luis was on top of her, using the strength of his legs and his free hand to stop her from bucking and kicking out at him.

She opened her mouth to scream at him again, to demand he let go of her at once but nothing came out. Her tongue had become a stranger in her own mouth, unable to form the needed words.

Far from recoiling at being trapped in his hold, she felt the fight inside her morph into something equally ferocious but of a shockingly different flavour as his scent found its way into her bloodstream. Pulses flickered to life, electricity zinging over and through her.

His dark hazel eyes hovered only inches above her own, staring down at her with an intensity that made her chest expand and her abdomen contract.

'Are you going to behave yourself now, *bonita*?' he asked with a husky timbre she'd never heard before. A fresh pulse of heat ripped through her, filling her blood and her head with the fuzziest, dreamiest of sensations.

She could not tear her eyes away…

'Make me.' Her whispered words came unbidden from a voice that belonged to someone else.

Their gazes stayed locked until she found herself staring at the sensuous mouth she had so yearned to kiss.

And then that mouth fitted against her own and claimed her in a hard, ruthless kiss that sent her head and her senses spinning.

All her defences were stripped away from the first crush of his lips. Her mind emptied of everything except this moment, the heat that engulfed her… It *filled* her, from the tips of her toes all the way up, snaking into every crevice of her being.

With a greed she hadn't known existed within her, she kissed him back, wrapping her arms around his neck and cradling his head with her hands, digging her fingers through his hair to his scalp.

She had dreamed of kissing Luis for close to eight years. On cold nights she had imagined him lying beside her and keeping her warm with that hulking, magnificent body.

She had never imagined it could be like this. Warm? Her body had become a furnace, desire running on liquid petroleum in her very core. The heat of his kisses fuelled it beyond anything fantasy could evoke. His dark, chocolatey taste, the thickness of his tongue playing against her own, the weight of his hands roaming down her sides... those fantasies had been dull compared to this giddy, urgent reality.

Scratching her nails down the nape of his strong neck, her fingers had slipped under the collar of his T-shirt when a door into the sky lounge opened.

In the breath of a moment reality reasserted itself.

Wrenching her mouth away, she turned her face from him and saw a pair of legs exiting the room as whoever had walked in on them left abruptly.

The ignobility of the situation they had been found in was starkly apparent.

She snatched her hands away from his skin and bucked against him. 'Get *off* me.'

The sensuous lips pulled into a smile as Luis levered himself back up.

The moment he was upright, Chloe twisted herself off the sofa and fell in a graceless heap onto the floor.

She stared at him, wishing she could crawl away and hide for ever.

Chloe had been kissed before. She might be a virgin but she wasn't completely innocent. She'd experimented like everyone else but nothing she had done—which admittedly wasn't much—had been anything like this.

This was something else.

This kiss had come directly from heaven.

She had to remember it had been delivered by the devil himself.

'You did that on purpose,' she said in a breathless voice that made her wince. It was no consolation that Luis's breathing was as ragged as her own.

He arched a dark brown eyebrow. 'Kissed you?'

'You knew someone was going to walk in,' she hissed, grasping for excuses, anything to negate what she had just experienced. 'You wanted us to be caught like that to discredit me.'

What madness had taken control of her?

She imagined that within minutes their passionate embrace would be known by the entire crew, including the captain, who had locked himself in the bridge when she'd been seeking help to escape. They would all conclude that they had been right to deny her help. They would never take her entreaties seriously.

'I have many talents but mind control is not one of them.'

He could have fooled her. She would swear he'd just used a form of mind control. Something in his eyes, a magnetism, it had hypnotised her. It must have. Something that would explain the madness that had possessed her.

'I kissed you because you asked it of me.'

'I did *not*.' Scrambling to her feet, she smoothed her T-shirt over her belly, trying desperately to look composed on the outside even if on the inside she had turned into a hormonal, blubbering mess.

'What was *"make me"*, if not a challenge to kiss you?' He spread his arms across the back of the sofa in a nonchalant fashion that made her fingers itch all over again to smack him.

'It was not a challenge.' She was painfully aware her cheeks must be the colour of tomatoes.

Her lips had tingled for him. They still did.

His gaze stayed unwaveringly on hers. '*Bonita*, your eyes begged for my kiss. You kissed me back. You ran your fingers through my hair. Faking virginal outrage does not change any of that.'

'Shut up.'

'You blush like a virgin too.'

'I said, *shut up.*' Storming to the bar, Chloe grabbed the first bottle that came to hand and poured a hefty measure into a glass.

She felt his eyes watching her every move.

'*Dios*, you're not, are you?'

'Not what?' She took a large sip hoping whatever the potent liqueur was would numb her insides.

'A virgin.'

The fiery liquid halfway down Chloe's throat spluttered back out of her.

'You *are.*'

The sudden fascination in his voice made her want to hurl the remnants of her glass at him. Instead she tipped them into her mouth and forced herself to swallow.

Oh, wow, it *burned.*

She coughed loudly and blinked back the tears produced by her burning throat, hating the amusement she found in his gaze.

'Being a virgin is nothing to be ashamed of,' he said when she had herself back under control. 'And I would go easy with that—that's Cuban rum. It's very potent.'

Staring at him insolently, she poured herself another measure. Now the burn had abated she was left with a pleasant after-taste. 'I'm not a virgin. I've slept with tons of men. Many more and I'll be on the same number of conquests as you.'

Luis ignored her gibe. Her lie was written all over her flaming-red face and trembling hands.

His heart twisted.

It had never occurred to him that Chloe was a virgin. And why would it? She was twenty-five, an age when a person would have had a number of lovers in their life. This was the twenty-first century. Women were as entitled to take lovers as men were. He had never met a woman who hadn't embraced the liberation that came with it.

Until now.

He thought of how her cheeks had always turned crimson when he saw her at the theatre, the look in her eyes when he had rubbed his nose against hers...

'It explains a lot,' he mused, shaking his head, incredulous at the turn of events since she had stormed back into the sky lounge.

Their kiss... It had exploded out of nowhere.

One moment he had been restraining her, the

next their mouths were locked together, their hands burrowing hard enough to dig through flesh.

There had been no finesse. They had come together in a brief fusion of unleashed desire.

'Because I refused a nightcap?' She tossed the drink down her throat with a grimace. 'That's called having self-respect.'

'If you've had a *ton* of lovers, why refuse to sleep with me? Your self-respect would already have been out of the window if that's what you were hoping to preserve.'

'Maybe I just didn't fancy you enough to come back to your house? Maybe I didn't want to be another conquest in a long line of many.'

'If it's the former then you lie—your body language is very expressive, *bonita*.' Her blush was delicious.

She was delicious.

Her sweetness lingered on his tongue, the softness of her skin still alive on the pads of his fingers.

'If the latter, why worry about being a conquest when you have such a long list of your own?'

She poured herself some more rum. 'I do not have to explain myself.'

'I'm merely curious as to why such a sensual woman would deny herself the pleasure that makes the world turn around.'

'Pleasure—sex—counts for nothing. There are far more important things. Like loyalty,' she added pointedly.

'We are already agreed on the importance of loyalty but only someone with minimal experience would deny that sex is an important part of life, especially someone who has slept with *tons* of men.' He hooked an ankle over his knee and enjoyed the fresh batch of colour flaming her cheeks.

Her presence alone invigorated him. He'd felt a lifting of his spirits when he'd first stepped into the sky lounge and surprised her with his presence. The hammers that had pounded at his head when she'd disappeared on her quest for escape had been driven out again with one look on her return.

Their kiss had pumped something else inside him, a buzzing in his veins.

He remembered their date; that buzz had been

with him throughout it then too, an electric charge in his cells that had driven out the strains of his daily life and the weight that always seemed to be pressing on his shoulders.

'If you have slept with the number of men you claim you have and can still state that sex is unimportant then that would suggest you have either been doing it wrong or have been picking the wrong partners.'

'Is this where you tell me that having sex with you will awaken me to all the things I've been missing out on?' She rolled her eyes with a snort.

Laughter bubbled up his throat. Chloe had the face of an angel, the body of a siren and a melodious voice that sang to a man's loins. It had only taken him so long to become fully aware of it because of all the years he'd seen her as a child.

He doubted there was a heterosexual man who'd met her and not felt a twinge of awareness for her.

Had she really, as he now strongly suspected, turned down every man who'd shown an interest in her?

And if so, why?

'Close your eyes, *bonita*, and let your senses

guide you. What do you taste? It is the chemistry between us seeping into the air we breathe.'

If he hadn't suspected before that they had the potential to be incredible together, their brief, furious kiss had proven it.

She scowled as she poured herself more rum with a still-shaking hand. 'The only thing I can taste is the hot air you keep spouting every time you open your mouth.'

His laughter came out as a roar.

No wonder he felt so invigorated to be with her. Chloe had a zest about her that he fed off. She'd always had it.

He remembered seeing a glimpse of the woman she'd become when they'd celebrated her seventeenth birthday at the chateau mere weeks before her mother had died. She'd been a gangly teenager still growing into her face, the beauty so evident today nothing but potential back then.

She was a full decade younger than the rest of them but her indefatigable spirit during those awful months her mother had been dying before their eyes had been inspiring.

Chloe had been the one to keep everyone's spirits lifted. She had kept that smile on her face during the worst of times, never once letting her mother see the pain that had been hidden behind it, always turning the stone over to find the ruby underneath. She would speed from school to the hospital and later Benjamin's newly bought chateau where Louise had ended her days, armed with cosmetics and other feminine products, doing her mother's hair, massaging her feet, painting her nails, all the little tactile things that had shown her love. All of it conducted with a smile and that raucous laugh that had lifted everyone and pulled them all together in a web of joyous love.

Her hidden pain had only come out at the funeral.

The memory of her tears soaking into his shirt that day and the tremulous look in the baby-blue eyes staring at him now cut the laughter from Luis's lips.

Whatever mistakes he had made, he had done his best by Chloe and her family. He had loved her mother and her brother. He had loved all of them. That she could believe him capable of using that awful time for his own financial gain sliced like a dagger through his chest.

Hindsight gave him much to regret but the past was the past. It was the future he had to think of and that future involved Chloe by his side as his wife.

Sentimentality had no part in it.

She held the glass of rum to her lips. 'Does the possibility of me being a virgin not make you pause and think that what you're doing is wrong on so many levels that Dante's *Inferno* would have run out of space for you?'

'You are thinking ahead to us sharing a bed?' he asked, fresh sensation awakening in his loins as he brushed the last of the memories away.

'*Never.* I despise you.' She swallowed the rum in one hit.

'No, *bonita*, you hate that you desire me.'

'Don't tell me what I feel,' she snapped, pouring herself yet another glass. By Luis's estimate she had drunk over a third of the bottle in a very short time.

She downed it and fixed her eyes on him with a glare. 'I will *never* be yours,' she repeated, then gave a hiccup. Then another.

She reached for the bottle again.

'Are you sure that's wise?'

'Stop telling me what to…' another hiccup '…do.' Her hand went to her mouth. When she next looked at him her face had lost much of its colour.

He leaned forward, preparing to get to his feet. 'Feeling woozy?'

'No.' As if to prove her point she took two steps towards him but then stopped herself and grabbed hold of the bar.

'I did suggest you eat something. All that rum on an empty stomach…'

She swallowed then took some long, deep breaths before raising her chin and studiously walking to the nearest seat. Seated, she gripped onto the arms of the sofa she had put herself into and flashed a grimace at him. 'See? I'm fine.'

He raised a brow, torn between guilt at driving her to attacking the rum, admiration at her refusal to submit and amusement at the hangover he was certain was coming for her.

'Ready for some food now? A bread roll or some toast to soak the alcohol?'

Her beautiful, stubborn mouth opened. He could see the refusal ready to be thrown at him. But then the mouth closed and she seemed to shrink a little into the chair.

When she met his eye there was a glimpse of vulnerability in her returning stare that made his heart twist and his chest tighten.

She gave a short jerky nod. 'Just something light, please. I think I'm suffering from seasickness.'

Dios, she was amazing. Clearly inebriated as she had suddenly become, she still had the wit to try and turn it to her advantage.

'You suffer from seasickness?' he asked with faux sympathy.

She gave another nod. 'You should put me on dry land…unless you want me to vomit all over your new toy?'

'That is certainly something for me to consider,' he said gravely.

'I would consider it quickly if I were you or I won't be…hic…responsible for the consequences.'

'If it gets too bad I will get the ship's doctor to give you something. He has a supply of anti-nausea injections and pills for such an eventuality. In the meantime, I'm sure some food will help.'

Whistling, Luis strolled out of the sky lounge with the weight of Chloe's glare burning into his back.

CHAPTER FIVE

'Feeling better?'

'A little.'

'Still seasick?'

'Yes. Very seasick.'

Luis's cynical laughter ringing behind her ear sounded like a hammer to Chloe's brain.

She tightened her grip on the railing and kept her gaze fixed on the clear waters surrounding her. She had been standing at the front of the yacht for almost an hour, inhaling the fresh air to clear her banging head.

She knew she wasn't fooling him with her woes of seasickness.

Faking seasickness had been better than admitting she was slightly—okay, a touch more than slightly—drunk.

The last time she'd consumed that much alcohol she'd been living in London but that had been spread over a number of hours, never in such a short space of time.

She had never drunk as much black coffee as she had since either. Cut her and she was quite sure she would bleed caffeine.

She'd needed the alcohol's numbness to smother the tortured emotions that had been engulfing her. There was nowhere to escape, nowhere to flee the heat his kiss had generated and her excruciating embarrassment at being called out as a virgin.

How had he known that? *Did* he have psychic powers? Or had he been with so many women that he could tell an innocent by one kiss?

Reaching the age of twenty-five a virgin was just something that had happened, not something intentional and not something she had been embarrassed about before.

When she'd moved to London months before turning nineteen to take on her apprenticeship with the ballet company, all the freedom in the world had suddenly been in her lap. It hadn't been that she'd been denied her freedom before then; she'd lived with her father and stepmother for the year following her mother's death and neither of them had shown the slightest concern for her whereabouts, then she'd spent a year living with her brother, who had watched her closely but never stifled her. This had been a different freedom.

Her whole life had opened itself out to her, unanswerable to anyone. She had embraced that freedom with gusto.

She had loved her life in London. Living in a shared house with three other young women had meant lots of partying and a growing number of friends. Long days and long nights, young enough to burn the candle at both ends without any ill effects...yes, she had loved her life back then but not as much as her housemates had.

Rarely a morning had gone by when Chloe would go downstairs for breakfast and not find a man or two in the kitchen, different faces on a seemingly daily basis. She'd recoiled from such casual hook-ups for herself. She'd dated though, even kissed a few of them, but nothing more. The mechanism inside her friends that allowed them to discard their inhibitions and embrace sex whenever and wherever they could seemed to be faulty in her.

'You're too choosy,' her best friend Tanya had drunkenly told her one night. And she had been right. Chloe loved her male friends but she did not trust them. There were only two men she'd trusted. One was her brother, the other had been Luis.

She hadn't deliberately sought Luis out. When she had seen his ballet company advertising for a costume maker she'd been ready for a fresh challenge.

To discover her old teenage feelings for him had been merely dormant and then to find her resurgent desire reciprocated had been both exhilarating and terrifying.

She had spent the past two months consoling herself that at least she hadn't accepted his offer of a nightcap.

Everything she had believed about Luis for her whole life had been torn asunder.

He had ripped her misplaced trust to shreds.

And now she knew her self-consolation had been pointless too. She still desired him. She'd been pinned beneath him and instead of kicking him where it hurt she had melted for him.

Worse, he knew it too.

'You will be glad to know we will be docking within the hour,' he said nonchalantly placing his hand on the railing beside her.

Chloe's heart leapt, although whether that was at his sudden closeness or his announcement she could not be sure.

She stepped to the side, away from him, not quite daring to get her hopes up. 'You're going to let me go?'

'No, *bonita*. I'm taking you to my island.'

'*Your* island?'

'*Sí*. I bought it with the yacht.'

'You bought an island to trap me on as well as a yacht?' Her leaping heart sank in dismay as that tiny glimpse of freedom disintegrated.

'They came as a package. I had intended to stay at sea a few more days so that Marietta's furniture could be moved out but necessity has brought the schedule forward. I have a video conference in the morning. This yacht, as magnificent as she is, was designed as a pleasure vessel and does not yet have business facilities.'

A swell of something hot and rabid pulsed in her chest. 'You bought the island off Marietta too?'

'I've met her a few times socially—I'd attended

one of her parties on this yacht. When I learned where you were hiding and its close proximity to her island, I called her with my offer. The stars aligned for me that day, *bonita*.'

'If the stars aligned for you then God knows what torturous trick they were playing on me,' she whispered bitterly.

'What can be torturous about staying in paradise?'

'How about that I'll be staying in it against my will?'

His tone became teasing. 'At least you won't have to worry about seasickness.'

She tightened her hold on the railing and breathed in deeply. 'How long will we stay there?'

'You will stay until you agree to marry me. It really is very simple. Marry me and then we return to the real world.'

'The real world where I'll be your wife?'

'That's what marriage means, *bonita*. We marry, make some public appearances together to kill the heinous rumours and speculation being spread about me and my brother and then you go free. It will all be over. You will be free to resume your life and your brother will not have to spend *his* life watching his back for my vengeance. You can put an end to all of it. The power is in your hands.'

She stared down at Luis's hand, tanned and huge, holding the rail so loosely beside her own. *That* was a powerful hand, in more ways than one. It could swallow her own hand up.

If she didn't find a way out of this mess *he* would swallow her whole.

But this was a mess she didn't know how to resolve. She *couldn't* marry him.

Just having him there beside her, that masculine scent her nose hungered for catching in the breeze and filtering through her airways had her senses dancing with awareness.

But she couldn't stop her eyes darting back to those hands. They had pinned her wrists together without any effort at all.

Her abdomen clenched, warmth flooding her to imagine them touching her again…

She would not let that happen. Luis would never lay a finger on her body ever again and she would not allow herself to touch him either, whether she married him or not.

Suddenly it occurred to her that Luis was taking her to an island which meant new people, telephone lines—her phone had no means of communication on this yacht—and transport. Which all meant potential escape routes...

But what if he meant it about ending the feud with her brother? Her being trapped here in his power proved the lengths Luis would go to.

She could laugh at her naivety. As if she could trust a word Luis said, after everything he had done.

Gathering all the raging emotions zipping within her and squashing them into a tight ball, Chloe twisted to look him right in the eye and then immediately wished she hadn't.

She was trapped, in more ways than one.

All she could do was gaze into the dark hazel eyes staring at her with a force that made her stomach melt and her fingers itch to touch him all over again.

Those strong fingers she had only moments ago stared at with a strange aching feeling reached out to smooth a lock of her hair behind her ear.

'Marry me, *bonita*,' he whispered, then craned his head towards her and brushed those sensuous lips over hers.

Chloe's feet were still stuck to the decking when he pulled his hand away and strode back into the sky lounge. It wasn't until the door closed behind him that the strange fog-like thing that had happened in her head filtered out to be replaced with anger, at Luis and especially at herself.

So much for never allowing him to touch her again. She had barely lasted a minute from making that vow.

In disgust, she wiped her still-tingling mouth with the back of her hand.

Must try harder, she thought grimly as she stared back out to sea with a heart still thumping madly.

Chloe came to a stop on soft golden sand upon which dreams were made. In front of her, gleaming like a Maharaja's palace under the descending sun, set in an island within the island, was a whitewashed mansion with a terracotta roof from which even more fantastical dreams were made.

They had been met off the yacht by a skinny boy of around ten, who skipped alongside her, clearly bursting with excitement. In rapid-fire

English he happily told Chloe that he was the caretakers' son and had lived on the island his whole life.

His cheerful presence was a welcome respite from the turbulence she had been through that day, although did nothing to lessen the coils knotted tightly in her belly.

Luis walked some way behind them, deep in conversation with the yacht's captain. She felt his presence like a spectre.

Determined to blank him out while she could, she tried hard to concentrate on the child's chattering while taking in everything around her.

The closer she got to the palace-like structure, the more she realised her initial thoughts were an illusion. What she'd thought was one palatial villa was a complex of interlinked homes around one huge main house nestled with high palm trees and traversed by the longest swimming pool she had ever seen, snaking the perimeter and weaving between the individual beautiful buildings. Only as she crossed a bridge over the swimming pool did she realise it was a saltwater pool filled with marine life that must feed directly from the sea.

Following the wide path, she saw what was undoubtedly a traditional pool snaking the main house like a moat, more bridges leading to the smaller homes.

Chloe sighed with pleasure then hated herself for it, immediately following her self-castigation with the thought that it was better to be locked away in paradise than in a cell.

She'd thought the complex she was staying on in Grand Bahama was paradise. This was nirvana.

'Who else lives on the island?' she asked the boy when she could get a word in.

His nose wrinkled but before he could answer, Luis got into step beside her.

'No one,' he answered cheerfully, the look in his eyes telling her clearly that her hopes of finding escape off this island were as futile as her hopes of finding help on the yacht. 'I will bring new staff in soon.'

'Jalen!' a loud, harsh voice called out. 'Come here.'

The little boy's skinny frame froze momentarily before he pulled himself together and ran off, back over the bridge they had just crossed to a scowling, weather-beaten man who'd emerged from the side of the main villa.

'Who's that?' Chloe asked, following Jalen with her eyes.

'Rodrigo. His father.'

She looked at Luis and found his gaze was also following the boy. 'The caretaker?'

He nodded, his attention still on the boy. 'He looks after the island with his wife, Sara.'

'Jalen said they've been here for a long time.'

'Sara's lived here for ever. Her parents were the caretakers before she took over.' There was a grimness to his tone.

Chloe looked back at Jalen. He'd reached his father and his head was bowed. He was obviously on the receiving end of a scolding. 'What do you think he did wrong?'

'I have no idea. I met the family three days ago when I took possession of the island. I know nothing about them.' Luis shook his head and pushed his attention away from the young boy and back to the beautiful woman at his side.

Small boys always pushed their luck. It was a parent's job to discipline them. Just because

Luis's father's methods of discipline had been extreme did not mean Rodrigo used the same methods.

But when he met Chloe's gaze he saw the same concern ringing out from her as needled in his own skin.

'Where do they live?' she asked.

'In one of the staff cottages at the back of the main house.' He pushed Jalen and Rodrigo more firmly from his head. He would have plenty of time to observe them interact and, he was sure—hoped—he would find the father-son relationship that he had spent so many years wishing for.

His own history was not others' reality. That was a truth he had always been aware of.

Luis had long ago accepted that there had been something in his genetic make-up that had triggered his father's violence towards him, something dirty and rotten.

It had to be inherent otherwise Javier would have been on the receiving end of it too. He'd never bought Javier's reasoning that he'd got away with only mild chastisement and a rumpled shake of the hair because their father had looked at Javier's face and seen a mirror of himself.

There was no denying that Javier had inherited their father's looks while Luis had inherited a masculine version of their mother's, and there was no denying that only Luis had been Yuri's whipping boy, right until the day their father's drunken, jealous rage had turned on their mother.

His father had served ten years of his sentence for killing his mother. A year after his release he'd died of pancreatic cancer. Luis sincerely hoped he'd suffered every minute of his death.

Dios, would it always be like this? Would he be condemned to a life where every time he saw a father chastise his child the memories of his own childhood would smack him in the face afresh?

Would the past ever set him free?

Strolling along another bridge that led to the door of a pretty villa, he said to the woman who could kill the demons from the past affecting his future, 'This will be your villa while we're here...'

She raised a startled eyebrow. 'I get my own villa?'

'Did you want to share one with me?' he mocked, glad to be back on familiar ground with her.

'No!'

He pushed the door open and winked at her.

This was better. Flirtation and teasing. Let it flow between them. Let it warm the coldness that had settled in his veins.

'If you change your mind, I will be in the villa next door.'

'Get over yourself.'

'I'd rather have you over me but I can wait.'

'You'll be waiting a long time.'

He gazed at her flushed cheeks and smiled. 'We shall see.'

She scowled but there wasn't the force behind it that had been there throughout the day.

She had made no effort to step into her new home. 'Are you not going to live in the main house?'

'Not until Marietta's possessions have been shipped out. I'll show you around it tomorrow but, for now, I have a conference call to plan for and I need to make sure everything's set up. Tonight, *bonita*, you get to amuse yourself. Sara will be with you shortly and will go through everything. She knows the island better than I do and has arranged the villa for your arrival. If there is anything you're not happy with, take it up with her.'

'You're not scared I might try and escape?'

He laughed. 'There is no escape. And no rescue, if that's what you're thinking. This island is an unnamed dot on the map.'

'What about the ship that's coming for Marietta's stuff?'

He noticed the darkening of her eyes as she spoke Marietta's name. It was the same darkening he'd noticed earlier.

'She's in no hurry for it.'

'I can hijack the yacht.'

'I'm afraid not. Captain Brand's taken it back to the mainland. He will return in a week and then he will marry us.'

'He can't.'

'He's a recognised officiate.'

'What does that mean?'

'That he can marry us.'

'But I haven't agreed to marry you!'

'You will and the sooner you accept it and say

yes, the sooner we can marry and the sooner this nightmare will be over for the both of us.'

He could manage a week away from the business but, he had realised earlier, no longer than that. He was still in communication with those he needed to communicate with but this island, for all its beauty, was cut off from civilisation as he knew it. For this to be a true holiday home he would need to purchase a helicopter to be permanently manned there and possibly get a landing strip put in and buy a smaller version of his private jet.

He was confident he would gain Chloe's acceptance to marry him in the seven-day deadline he had imposed.

He could sense her resolve failing her. She knew there was no escape. If she wanted to leave the Caribbean she would have to marry him.

She was the reason he was having to scramble together a conference call the next morning to salvage a deal that had been in the bag and stop the business he and his brother had worked so hard for from crumbling around them.

Before she could respond, a slender, tired-looking woman with frazzled hair crossed the bridge to them.

Luis shook Sara's hand then introduced her to Chloe. 'Please see that Miss Guillem has everything she needs,' he said, then turned back to Chloe.

Was it his imagination or was that panic resonating from those beautiful blue eyes?

He reached out a hand to stroke her soft cheek.

The pupils of her eyes pulsed at his touch.

'I will find you after my conference call tomorrow,' he said. 'Until then, stay out of trouble.'

Chloe watched him walk away with the strangest desire to call him back.

She managed a small smile at Jalen's mother and was relieved to receive a warm, if tired, smile back.

The villa she was shown into was charmingly beautiful if a little old-fashioned and fitted with its own kitchen and all the amenities a woman could want. The swimming pool curled past the bottom of the pretty garden her living room opened out to.

'I hear you've always lived on the island,' Chloe said when Sara was about to leave.

Chloe *hated* being alone at the best of times but with her head so full of the day's events, so full of Luis, the thought of only her own company terrified her.

Sara nodded and put her hand on the door. 'I was born here.'

'What's Marietta like?' she couldn't resist asking.

Why she couldn't stop imagining the mystery woman she could not begin to fathom but the name had lodged itself in her head like a spike digging into it.

Luis had bought Marietta's yacht and island off her and taken possession of them both in mere days. He'd met her socially.

Chloe knew all about Luis and his sociability. His party-loving ways were legendary. She remembered the leaked photos of his thirtieth birthday party, a joint event with his twin at which her brother had, naturally, been a guest. Someone had captured pictures of Luis dancing, beer in hand, surrounded by a hive of semi-naked women, all with their attention fixed firmly on him.

A quote in the paper by an unnamed source

had described it as the party of the decade. To the question of which of the beauties Luis had ended up with, the answer had been, 'Knowing Luis, it could have been all or any of them.'

Recalling that picture made her want to vomit.

Had Marietta been at that party? Had she been one of those beauties draped all over him?

Sara's face lit up into a smile that momentarily transformed her tired features into beauty. 'She's an amazing woman.'

Later, alone on her villa's veranda after a light supper eaten alone, Chloe sat under the starry night sky nursing a glass of water.

Other than the crickets chirruping madly to each other, the silence was absolute. There was no sign of life from the villa next door, no lights, no sound.

She could be the only person on this earth.

Luis must still be in the main villa preparing for his video conference.

She should be happy to be rid of him, not re-living their kiss for the fiftieth time.

Dieu, now she was alone with her thoughts it

was *all* she could think about, their lips and bodies fused together and the *heat* that engulfed her.

She rubbed her eyes and breathed even more deeply.

Why did any of this have to happen?

If Luis and Javier had been straight with Benjamin all those years ago instead of luring him into a lie then she would…

Would what?

She would have gone on that second date with Luis. She would have accepted his offer of a nightcap. She would have let him kiss her. And then she would have let him make love to her.

And then he would have broken her heart.

In a way, he had broken it already through his treachery to her brother and all the memories that had been shattered as a result.

He had a ruthless streak in him she would never have guessed ran so deep.

But, as her memories continued to torture her, she thought back to his vehement denials of treachery.

Now she had a little distance from him and could think without his magnetic presence disturbing her equilibrium, she couldn't help but wonder if there was some truth in his defence of himself.

As a child Luis had been her favourite visitor to their home. She had loved it when he and Javier had come to stay, had a strong memory of climbing to the top of the fifteen-foot tree at the bottom of their garden but then losing her nerve and being too scared to climb back down.

She had sat at the top of it, crying her head off, terrified of the drop, which to her five-year-old self had looked petrifying.

Luis had been the one to haul himself up and get her down. She had clung to him like a limpet but he had got them both down safely. She had hero-worshipped him for that. His steady presence when her mother had become ill had been such a comfort to all of them. His visits had brightened her mother's mood, invigorated her brother and made her own heart lighten a little.

Had that *all* been a lie? Had twenty-five years' worth of memories all been false or distorted?

And then she thought of the social media comments he had mentioned, the sick ones that had equated Freya leaving Javier out of fear of ending up like Clara Casillas. Fear of ending up murdered at Javier's hands.

Had there been cruel comments aimed at Luis too?

The rustle of movement nearby pulled her back to the present, a door being closed softly.

Footsteps crunched and, although their individual gardens gave them privacy, she knew in her bones that Luis had stepped outside into his villa's garden.

Chloe held her breath. Her heart beat maniacally beneath her ribs, all her senses pinging to life. The knots in her stomach had tightened to become a painful ache inside her.

Could he sense her, feet away, separated only by the hedgerow filled with an abundance of beautifully scented flowers?

A short while later she heard the distant splash of water. Luis had gone for a midnight swim.

Still holding her breath, she took that as her cue to bolt back inside.

Her head felt hot and thick when she slipped under the cool bed sheets a short while later. A riot of images flashed behind her closed eyes that no amount of trying could dispel.

Luis swimming.
Luis naked.
Luis, Luis, Luis…

CHAPTER SIX

THE IMAGE OF Luis swimming naked was the first thing Chloe saw in her mind's eye when she awoke the next morning after a turbulent night that had not involved much in the way of sleep.

Throwing the bed sheets off, she hurried into the bathroom and took a long shower, washing the images—which weren't even images, just something conjured by her pathetic imagination—away.

With a towel wrapped around her torso and another wrapped around her head, she opened the dressing-room door to see what clothes had been brought in for her. Inside she found a collection of beach and summer wear, all in a variety of sizes.

She supposed she should feel grateful that Luis had made sure there would be something that would fit her. She wasn't the easiest of women to dress. At five foot eight, she was taller than average. If not for her breasts, she would be considered slender. Her breasts had been the envy of her friends when she'd been a developing teenager. She'd always considered them to be a nuisance. Dresses were a nightmare to buy, always a compromise between fitting from the waist down or the waist up. If she wanted them to fit the rest of her without looking as if she were wearing a tent, she was forced to cut the circulation of her breasts off. The times she found a dress she liked and that fitted perfectly she would buy it in all the available colours.

She'd been wearing one of those dresses in the Madrid coffee shop the day she had seen Luis through the window, she suddenly remembered, hit afresh with the liquid sensation she had experienced as their eyes had met and, for the very first time, she had seen interest in his eyes.

The date that had followed had been the best evening of her life. She hadn't wanted it to end.

It had taken all her willpower to get into the cab and return to her apartment without him.

Inhaling deeply, she selected a blue bikini and covered it with a denim skirt that fell to mid-thigh and a black T-shirt, both of which fitted well.

She left her damp hair loose, put the coffee on

as Sara had shown her and opened the front door to the glorious bright Caribbean sunshine.

As she had promised, Sara had left a tray of food there for her. Sitting next to the tray and looking straight at her was a two-inch-long gecko.

Chloe crouched down to look properly at its cuteness. 'You are adorable,' she said, smiling at the reptile that appeared unfazed to have a strange woman making cooing noises at it.

'Stay where you are,' she told it, leaving the door open as she backed into the villa.

She'd left her bag on the dining table and quickly upended the contents to find her phone.

Her intention to take a picture of the cute gecko came to nothing when she stepped back out and found it gone.

With a sigh, she carried the tray in, shoving her mess to one side to fit it on the table.

About to put her phone down and pour the coffee out, she suddenly noticed the Wi-Fi icon showing itself.

Luis must have got the Wi-Fi working for her phone had logged in to it, no password needed for access.

She had no signal to make phone calls but she could communicate with the outside world.

The first thing she did, while absently chewing on a freshly baked croissant, too intent on her potential freedom to taste her food, was search the island's co-ordinates.

A message flashed up warning her that her Internet safety settings did not allow her to search this.

She tried again but to no avail. Equally, she found herself blocked from accessing her emails and social media.

She could scream.

Foiled again.

As always, Luis was two steps ahead of her.

Luis...

Remembering his claims about malevolent comments on the Internet, she wrote his and Javier's names into the search box.

Her search engine announced there were over two hundred thousand results.

She clicked on the first news article, a gossip piece about Freya and Benjamin's 'secret' wedding. She scrolled to the comments section.

Twenty minutes later she switched her phone

off and threw it onto the heap of stuff from her emptied beach bag, nauseated.

How could people write such things? And on public forums too?

She wished she could scrub her eyeballs out and cleanse them from the poison she had just subjected them to.

Had Luis read those comments?

She fervently hoped not. She hoped Javier hadn't either.

No one deserved hateful comments like that. No one should ever have to read faceless, anonymous opinions that they had evil in their eyes, were inherently bad, were secret psychopaths, were women-beaters, that they'd inherited their father's violence.

What the hell were the moderators of these news sites doing? she wondered angrily. How could they let such toxic bile onto their sites?

This was worse than she had imagined. A thousand times worse.

She closed her eyes as a memory hit her of when she'd been really young. It might have been the same summer she had got stuck in the tree. The Casillas twins and Benjamin had sat around her kitchen table playing a board game she'd been too young to join in with. She couldn't remember the game itself but vividly remembered the booming laughter that had echoed through the walls of her home, remembered stealing into the kitchen in the hope of sharing the array of snacks her mother had laid out for them. One of the boys—she wished she remembered which— had ruffled her hair and slipped her some crisps.

In her mind back then, the three had been giants fully grown in comparison to her puny self, but now she knew they'd been kids in frames their brains were trying to catch up with. Two of the three had been living with a trauma her own young brain had been unable to comprehend.

That those two vulnerable boys should have such spite aimed at them now made her heart ache.

Chloe was comfortable with the world at large questioning the Casillas brothers' business integrity but this…

This was sickening. This was personal.

She had never, would never, could never, have wanted this. Not for anyone but especially not for them.

* * *

Luis closed his laptop with an exasperated sigh.

The video conference with their Canadian partner had not gone well.

He had a bad taste in his mouth and was thankful his brother was thousands of miles away so he couldn't give in to the urge to punch him in the face.

'We do not have to explain ourselves to you,' Javier had said from his home office in Madrid. 'The litigation between ourselves and Benjamin Guillem is not a matter of gossip.'

'I am not a man who deals with gossip,' George had retorted, visibly affronted. 'But I am a man who needs to feel comfortable with who I do business with. The rumours are that you ripped Benjamin Guillem off on the Tour Mont Blanc development. If you cannot refute those rumours then I cannot be expected to put my name and money to this development with you.'

'We do not need your money,' Javier had said coldly.

'But you do need the access I can provide. Without my backing this project is dead in the water.'

That was when Luis had stepped in. 'The lit-igation between us is sealed for confidentiality reasons. However, I can assure you Benjamin Guillem was paid every cent owed under the terms of the contract we all signed seven years ago.'

'I'm afraid your assurances are not enough. I will need to see that contract and the full ac-counts for the project if I am to proceed.'

'If our word is not good enough for you then it is *us* who needs to rethink this deal,' Javier had retorted, ice seeping through every syllable. 'We will not do business with someone who takes the salacious word of the tabloid press over ours.'

And then his brother had cut himself off from the conference.

Luis had kept the deal on the table only by apol-ogising profusely and explaining the tremendous strain his brother was under.

A huge part of him had been tempted to tell George to take a hike and pull the plug on the project himself, write off the money they'd al-ready spent and the hours he'd spent as point man on it, but that would mean giving in.

His brother had since turned his phone off, no doubt taking himself off to pound the hell out of a punching bag as he always did when his anger got the better of him. Living with the shadow of their father's violence had affected them in different ways and it was in their own reactions to anger that they diverged the most. Javier closed himself off and showed his true emotions only to inanimate objects. Luis was as comfortable with anger as he was with pleasure. Harness it in the right way—a lesson learned by always doing the opposite of what his father would have done—and the anger could be used as fuel.

Javier might be prepared to throw in the towel but Luis was not. Why should they allow the business they had worked so hard for be destroyed? Was it not bad enough that their reputations were being destroyed, their names dragged through the mud?

He would not let it all go without a fight.

And from Chloe not the slightest bit of contrition.

He hadn't seen her since he'd shown her to the villa that would be her dwelling for the immediate future.

She had been on his mind every minute of her

absence, even during that damned video conference.

Fed up of the cloying walls of the room he'd turned into an office for himself, Luis left the main villa and headed over the moat to the beach.

His beach.

This whole island, bought as an insurance policy to keep Chloe tied to his side, belonged to him.

Rolling his sleeves up, he welcomed the sun's rays onto his skin as his attention was caught by two figures on the golden beach...

Was that *music* he could hear?

He pulled his loafers off and stepped onto the soft sand, walking closer to the figures that revealed themselves to be Chloe and Jalen. They were dancing...or something that looked like dancing, the kind of moves the more drunken revellers at his parties would make as the night wore on, body popping, robot moves; the pair of them facing each other having some kind of dance-off, oblivious to his presence.

Not wanting to disturb them, he sat on the sand, enraptured with what was playing out before him and enjoying the beat of the hip-hop music.

The longer he watched, the thicker his blood ran, awareness spreading like syrup through him.

This was the Chloe he knew, joyous, enjoying a spontaneous moment, her beautiful face lit up and glowing, her raven hair spraying in all directions and...*vaya*, that body.

After a good ten minutes of frenzied dancing, Chloe stopped and doubled over to massage the side of her stomach. By the grimace on her face she was the victim of a stitch.

She twisted slightly and that was when their eyes met.

After a long moment of hesitation, she turned away and said something to Jalen, who immediately looked at Luis, grabbed what was recognisably an old-fashioned boom-box and scarpered.

Slowly she trod barefoot to him, one hand holding her flip-flops, the other still massaging her side, breathing heavily, her eyes not leaving his face until she stood before him.

For a passage of time that seemed to last for ever, they stared wordlessly at each other until she took one last inhalation and sank onto the sand, lying flat on her back beside him, clearly exhausted.

'I didn't know you were into hip-hop,' he said wryly, bemusement and awareness laced together in his veins.

She gave a ragged laugh, her gaze fixed on the sky. 'Neither did I. Sara told me you were still on your conference call so I went for a walk and found Jalen.' She took a breath that turned into a groan. 'I'm shattered. I've become so unfit.'

He stared at the flat of her white stomach, exposed where her T-shirt had ridden up her midriff, and resisted the temptation to run a hand over it. 'Not from where I'm sitting.'

She followed his gaze with a flush creeping over her cheeks, then tugged the T-shirt down over her navel. 'Some ground rules. If I'm going to be your wife then no flirting.'

'My wife?' His heart jolted then set off at a thrum. 'You are agreeing to marry me?'

The breath she took before inclining her head lasted an age. *'Oui.'*

He studied the beautiful face that was no longer looking at him. 'What made you change your mind?'

The last time they had spoken Chloe had been vehement in her refusal. He'd known she would agree eventually but had been sure it would take a few more days for her to see reason.

'I read the comments you spoke of.' Her brow furrowed. When she continued, there was real anger in her voice. 'They are *vile*. How people can even think such things…it is beyond anything I have ever seen. To post them on public forums like that…? Vile, vile, vile.'

'Let me be sure I am understanding you correctly,' he said slowly. 'You are comfortable with my business and reputation suffering through your actions but take exception to mindless fools' comments on the Internet?'

Chloe turned her head to stare into the hazel eyes that were studying her with an expression she did not understand.

'Those comments are *vile*,' she repeated fiercely. It was the only word she could think of that fitted. 'You and Javier are not your parents. Your father's crimes are not yours. You have suffered enough from what your father did, you shouldn't have to suffer in this way too.'

Because in essence that was what the cruel, ignorant commentators were saying, that the apple didn't fall far from the tree and that Yuri

Abramova's violence had been inherited by his sons and that they must have used their wealth and power to cover it up.

Oh, it made her *rage*. The more she had thought about it over the morning, the greater her anger had grown, reaching a boiling point when she had bumped into Jalen walking around with his beloved boom-box on his shoulder.

The simple, uncomplicated innocence she had seen on his young face had been the exact tonic she had needed while she waited for Luis to be done with his video conference.

'You'd manipulated things so I would have been forced to marry you eventually but this made my mind up for me,' she said into the silence that had broken out, reminding herself of his actions that *were* reprehensible and deserving of her fury. She might be having doubts on whether he had intentionally ripped her brother off but that did not excuse what he had done to *her*. 'I don't want to be stuck in limbo here for the rest of my life.'

'Being forced to spend your life on these beautiful shores sounds like a real hardship.'

For some reason, the dryness of his tone tickled her funny bone. She covered her face with her hands so he couldn't see the amusement he'd induced.

She didn't want him to make her laugh. It hurt too much.

'Are you crying?'

'No, I'm holding back a scream.' A scream to purge all the torment building itself back up in her stomach.

'What was that? I can't hear you.'

Moving her hands away, she was about to repeat what she'd said when she found he'd shifted to lean over her, his face hovering above hers.

'Do you mind?' she snapped, frightened at the heavy rhythm her heart had accelerated to in the space of a moment.

'You want me to move?'

'Yes.'

A gleam pulsed in his eyes. 'Make me.'

Instead of closing her hand into a fist and aiming it at his nose as he deserved, Chloe placed it flat on his cheek.

An unwitting sigh escaped from her lips as she drank in the ruggedly handsome features she had dreamed about for so long. The texture of his skin was so different from her own, smooth but with the bristles of his stubble breaking through…had he not shaved? She had never seen him anything other than clean-shaven.

His face was close enough for her to catch the faint trace of coffee and the more potent scent of his cologne.

Luis was the cause of all this chaos rampaging through her. She hated him so much but the feelings she'd carried for him for all these years were still there, refusing to die, making her doubt herself and what she'd believed to be the truth.

Her lips tingled, yearning to feel his mouth on hers again, all her senses springing to life and waving surrender flags at her.

Just kiss him…

Closing her eyes tightly, Chloe gathered all her wits about her, wriggled out from under him and sat up.

Her lungs didn't want to work properly and she had to force air into them.

She shifted to the side, needing physical distance, suddenly terrified of what would happen if she were to brush against him or touch him in any form again.

Fighting to clear her head of the fog clouding

it, she blinked rapidly and said, 'Do I have your word that your feud with Benjamin ends with our marriage?'

Things had gone far enough. For the sake of the three boys playing board games in her kitchen all those years ago, it was time to put an end to it.

'*Sí.* Marry me and it ends.'

She exhaled a long breath. '*D'accord.* If I am going to do this then there will be some ground rules. Our marriage will last as short a time as is possible.'

'Agreed.'

'And it will not be consummated.' Aware of her face going crimson again—*Dieu*, the heat she knew that was reflecting on her face was licking her everywhere—she scrambled to her feet.

A few inches of distance was not enough. Not when it came to Luis.

Two months of distance hadn't been enough.

How was she going to get through this? How was she going to cope with living with him, even if it was only for a few months, and keep her craving for him contained?

Somehow she would find a way. She could not give in to it; the dangers were too great.

This was *Luis* she was going to marry. The only man she had ever had feelings for, the man she had fallen for when she had been only seventeen, the only man other than her brother she had thought she could trust. Even if he'd spoken the truth about not deliberately betraying Benjamin, she knew it had only been the headiness of newly discovered desire that had made her want to trust him before.

She could never trust this ruthless, pleasure-seeking hedonist, not with her body and especially not with her fragile heart.

She could feel his eyes burning into her as he clarified, 'No sex?'

'Our marriage will be short and strictly platonic.' She strode away over the warm, fine sand, heading for the footpath that led back to the villas, needing to escape from him.

'Still holding on to your virginity?' he called after her.

She closed her eyes but didn't break stride.

She would not give him the satisfaction of a response.

The hairs on the back of her neck lifted as he easily caught up with her.

'Captain Brand's bringing the yacht back in six days. We will marry then. In the meantime, I'll get the pre-nuptial agreement drawn up.'

'What pre-nuptial agreement? If you think I want your money you're crazy.'

She didn't want *anything* from him.

'I am not interested in protecting my wealth, only my reputation and my future. You will sign a contract that forbids you from discussing our marriage.'

She stopped walking to stare at him in disbelief. 'You're going to put a gagging order on me?'

'I will not have you sharing with the world that you only married me because you were forced to.'

'Haven't you learned your lesson about stifling free speech from my brother?' she snapped, affronted. 'That injunction you put on him worked out so well, didn't it?' she added over her shoulder as she set off again.

The only reason she was agreeing to marry him was to stop the cruel things being stuck all over the Internet about him, not to add fuel to the fire.

Those cruel comments had hurt as much as if they had been personally directed at her. More.

As she was about to step onto the bridge over

the seawater moat, a strong hand snatched hold of her elbow and spun her around.

Where moments ago there had been a casual, almost lazily seductive look to his eyes, now there was a hardness. 'The injunction against Benjamin was necessary. He was a loose cannon—'

'Only because he felt you took advantage of him when our mother was dying.' She grabbed hold of the outrage that filled her, negating the growing guilt at what her actions had helped lead to. 'You can shout it as loudly as you like that you were going to give him that money but where's the evidence to back it up? It's been two months since the truth came out and all you have done is fight him in the courts. One phone call could have put an end to it.'

His hold on her elbow loosened but his angry face leant right into hers. 'Your brother hit us with the lawsuit two days after our confrontation when I was still furious at his accusations. You speak of betrayal, well, what about your brother's betrayal to friendship? He turned this into war, not us, and you were happy to join in with it. The only thing Javier and I are guilty of is protecting ourselves and if you would pull those damned blinkers from your eyes you would know it too, but you won't because then you would have to accept responsibility for *your* actions and accept that it suits you to cast me as the monster in the scenario.'

'In what possible way does it *suit* me to cast you as the monster?' she demanded to know as the rest of his accusations dragged through her skin as if they were attached to barbs.

She had never been *happy* to join her brother's side. She had been heartbroken for him...

But what if Benjamin had been wrong? What if his fury at the supposed betrayal had driven his actions to the point where reason was something no longer available to him?

'Because you, *bonita*, are running scared and have been since you ran off like a frightened virgin at the end of our date. Your brother's war with me was the excuse you needed.'

'*Excuse?* Listen to yourself! Your ego is so big you should buy another island to contain it in.'

Her heart thundering and her skin feeling as if the barbs of his words were being pulled through it, Chloe marched away. There was a cramp in her stomach far sharper than the stitch she'd had on the beach.

'Chloe!' His deep voice called after her in a growl but she didn't stop, upping her pace, trying her best to keep herself together through the burn of tears growing at the backs of her eyes and the cramp that had spread into her chest.

Hearing his assured footsteps closing in on her, she broke into a run, almost skidding over the swimming-pool moat bridge that led directly to her villa's path.

That she was doing exactly what he'd just accused her of—running scared—was something she understood on a dim, hazy level of her psyche but enough to propel her faster, a desperation to escape the eyes that saw too much and the emotions brimming inside her.

She pulled the door open with Luis only a couple of strides behind her and slammed it shut.

CHAPTER SEVEN

IF LUIS HAD been one step quicker the door would have slammed in his face.

He turned the handle, had pushed it open an inch when she threw her weight against the other side.

'Stay away from me,' she screamed through the closed door.

'Let me in or I will break it down,' he said with a calmness he did not feel. Right then he felt anything but calm.

He knew he should walk away and wait for Chloe to regain her composure but reason be damned. He would not allow her to walk away. She had run enough from him.

'I don't want anything to do with you.'

'Tough. Last chance, *bonita*. Open the door.'

His ultimatum was met with a choice of rude words.

He sighed heavily. 'Don't say I didn't warn

you.' And with that he used all his strength to barge the door open against the pressure Chloe exerted on the other side of it.

But he was by far the stronger of the two and in seconds he had it open.

She clearly had no intention of letting him in without a fight. As he stepped over the threshold, she hurled herself at him, pounding her fists against his chest, kicking him, her long raven hair whipping around her face as she threw curses at him.

He grabbed at her flailing arms and held her wrists tightly as she continued to struggle against him, clearly uncaring that her height and weight against his own made it a fight she could never win.

He managed to manoeuvre her so her back was to the wall and pulled her hands up and above her head and used the strength in his legs to pin her own and stop them kicking.

'Is this how it's going to be for the next few months?' he demanded, staring hard at the beautiful face glaring at him as if condensed with all the poison in the world. 'Is every cross word going to end with you running away or fighting me?'

Those gorgeous, voluptuous lips wobbled. The eyes firing loathing at him became stark, the fight dissolving out of her like a balloon struck with a pin.

'I don't know how to deal with it,' she whispered tremulously. 'It scares me.'

She no longer struggled against him.

His chest twisted to see the starkness of her fear. 'What scares you, *bonita*?'

She inhaled deeply through her nose. Her throat moved, her eyes pulsed and darkened, her lips parted…

And then those soft lips brushed against his and he was no longer pinning her to the wall but pulling her into his arms. The hands that had been hitting at him wrapped around his neck as their bodies crushed together and their mouths parted.

Her taste hit his senses like a knocked-back shot of strong liqueur. It played on his tongue, the sweet nectar that was Chloe's kisses, a flavour like no other.

Every cell in his body caught fire. The fever caught her too; there in the crush of her lips moving greedily against his own and the digging of her nails into his scalp and the hungry way her body pressed itself against him, an instantaneous combustion trapping them in a magnetic grip.

What was it with this woman that he responded to with such primal force? Chloe lit a fire inside him, fuelling it with kisses a man could use for sustenance. It was like nothing he had ever known before, as if all others before her had pitched him to a mere simmer.

Mouths clashing and devouring, Luis swept a hand up her back and under her cropped T-shirt, headily relishing the warm softness of her skin. Such beautiful, soft, feminine skin...

He found the ties of the bikini that contained the breasts he'd fantasised about for so long and pulled it undone. The bikini rose upwards as he traced his hand around her midriff and up to the newly released swell.

She gasped into his mouth as he cupped a breast far weightier than he'd imagined but soft like her lips and her skin. Her hands burrowed under the neck of his T-shirt and grabbed at the material.

The fire condensed into his loins. It burned, a pain like nothing he had felt before.

He'd never felt *any* of this before.

When he pressed his groin against her, his arousal ground against her abdomen, they moaned into each other's mouths before she wrenched her lips from his and rubbed her mouth against his cheek and tugged even harder at his T-shirt.

Together they scrambled to pull each other's T-shirts off and fling them to the floor, and then her arms were hooked back around his neck and her hot mouth devoured him all over again.

In a frenzy of kisses, Luis tugged the ties of her bikini at the back of her neck and whipped it off fully, discarding it without thought.

A pulsing thrill ripped through him at the first press of her bare breasts against his bare chest.

He wanted to taste those breasts and all her other hidden places and burrow his face in their softness.

Everything about Chloe was soft. Everything. And so utterly, amazingly feminine, the yin to his yang, soft where he was hard, porcelain wrapped in silk.

She was a woman like no other. Feisty, stubborn, smart, funny, all contained in a body that could make a grown man weep.

And she was going to be his wife.

Chloe's breaths were coming in pants. She could hear them, could feel herself make them but they seemed to be coming from somewhere else, from someone who was not herself.

She was not herself.

Her body had become something new, a butterfly emerging from its chrysalis, coaxed into the sunlight by the only man she had ever desired or wanted. She had become a vessel of nerve-endings, and they were all straining to Luis, all her hate and rage, pain and sorrow, turned on their head in the time it took for a coin to flip from heads to tails.

She was beyond caring about yet another self-made vow being broken.

If this was what broken promises felt like then she would break a thousand of them.

For two months she had focused on her passionate hatred of him. But her passion for him was more than hate, it always had been, and to deny this part of her feelings for him was like denying herself air. If she were to walk—run— away right now she would forget how to breathe.

Even her skin felt alive. Tendrils curled around her and through her, sensation burning deep inside.

She gasped again when he squeezed her bottom roughly and ground himself more tightly to her, the weight and size of his excitement pressed so deliciously against her loins sending newer, deeper sensations racing through her.

As he held onto her thighs and lifted her up, she wrapped her legs around him and kissed him even more deeply as he carried her to the bed in three long strides.

She had to keep kissing him. She needed the heat of his mouth on hers and that dark masculine taste firing into her senses to drive out the fears that had held her in its grip for too long.

What had there been to fear about *this*?

This was pleasure. Erotic, greedy and needy, not something to be frightened of but something to be embraced.

He placed her on the bed, her bottom on the edge, her arms still wrapped around him, Luis between her parted thighs.

He was the one to break the kiss.

She moaned her complaint and tried to resist as

he put a hand on her shoulder and gently pressed her back.

Her complaints died when she saw the darkness pulsating in his eyes as he lightly circled her breasts with his fingers, sending brand-new sensation over skin she hadn't known could be so sensitive. When he put his lips there too…

She closed her eyes to this new, intoxicating pleasure as he kissed each breast, flickering her nipples with his tongue.

So intense were the sensations that she was only dimly aware of his hands working on the buttons of her skirt and tugging it down her hips with her bikini bottoms, only fully aware that she had helped shed them by kicking them off when he brought his mouth back to her lips for another of his darkly passionate kisses.

When he put a hand to the womanly heart of her, an electric pulse charged through her, strong enough to lift her back into an involuntary arch. She drank his kisses while fresh, new pleasure assaulted her. His fingers gently but assuredly stroked and manipulated her, making her senses spin and rocket to an undiscovered dimension, and she cried a protest when his hand moved away from his heavenly doings and traced up and over her belly and covered her aching breasts.

Time slipped away and lost all meaning, thoughts dissipating to just one concrete thing: Luis.

This, here, now, was everything she had dreamed, everything she had…

Her eyes flew open.

Luis must have removed the rest of his clothing for suddenly she was conscious of a velvety thickness pressing against the apex of her thigh.

She gazed into the dark hazel eyes gazing so sensually into hers but with a question contained in them.

This is the point of no return, they said. *If you want this to stop then now is the time.*

Chloe would rather take a knife to the heart than stop. She had never wanted anything more than she did at this moment.

She placed her hand on his tightly locked jaw. It softened under her touch before he turned his face to kiss her palm.

Then she moved her arms round his back as he kissed her mouth again and put his hand between their conjoined bodies to take hold of himself and position himself at the most secret, hidden heart of her.

A hard, heavy pressure pushed against her but it was a pressure she welcomed; craved, his kisses no longer enough to satisfy the intense heat overwhelming every part of her.

Slowly he inched inside her with a careful tenderness to his movements that drove out what little fear still lived inside her. His lips brushed over her face and his hands stroked her hair, as he filled her bit by bit until he was fully inside her and their groins were locked together.

The newness of the sensation stunned her. She could feel *him*, inside her, over her, on her, two bodies fused together as one.

And then he kissed her again and began to move…and that was when she discovered the true meaning of pleasure.

Her legs wrapped around his waist, Chloe closed her eyes and let Luis guide her.

Luis.

Even with her eyes shut she could see him so clearly. The scent of his skin, a new muskiness to it, the smoothness of his skin, the bristles of the hairs of his chest brushing against her breasts…

He was her everything. Her pain, her pleasure, her desire, her hate, all blended together so there was only him.

Low in her most hidden part an intensity built, every slow thrust raising it higher and yet somehow deeper, everything inside her concentrating into one mass that finally reached a peak and exploded within her. Ripples pulsated and surged through her body with a strength that had her crying out. Pressing her cheek tightly to Luis's, she rode the waves of pleasure, the only thought echoing through her head that she didn't want this feeling to ever, ever leave her.

There was a wonderfully languid weight in Chloe's limbs she'd never experienced before, a mellow buzzing sensation in her veins. Luis's face was buried in her neck, his breath hot on her skin, fingers laced through hers.

Time seemed to have come to a stop.

She sighed when he raised himself up to stare down at her. She couldn't read the expression in his eyes but what she saw made her stomach melt and her heart clench.

His kiss was light but lingering before he climbed off the bed.

'Are you going?' she asked before she could stop herself.

A shutter came down in his eyes but his stare remained on hers. 'Do you *want* me to go?'

She hesitated before answering. She should want him to go. What they had just shared hadn't been planned—*Dieu*, had it not been planned—but the culmination of something that had fired into being months ago and been left to simmer. To tell him to leave would be an admission of regret and a denial of her own complicity.

She did not regret it. How could she? It had been the most intensely wonderful experience of her life.

And she would not be complicit in any more deceit.

There had been enough deceit between them to fill his yacht.

She swallowed. 'No.'

He inclined his head, a gleam returning in his eyes. 'Good. Because I'm not going anywhere apart from the bathroom to dispose of the condom.'

That made her blink.

When had he put that on?

She watched him stroll to the bathroom, unable to believe she hadn't noticed Luis slipping a condom on.

Wriggling under the bed sheets, she cuddled into the pillow, dazed that passion had engulfed her so acutely that it had swept her away to a place where she had lost all sense.

When Luis came back into the room in all his naked glory her heart skipped up into her mouth.

Her imagination of his naked form had not done him justice. He truly was a titan of a man, broad, muscular, bronzed, unashamed in his masculinity.

A smile curved on his lips as he strolled towards her and lifted the bed sheets to climb on top of her.

Elbows either side of her face, Luis gazed down at the face that had been like a spectre in his mind for so long, drinking in the expression in the baby-blue eyes, the flawless porcelain skin, the voluptuous lips that kissed like the softest pillow.

He dipped his head and kissed her softly. 'Do you regret making love?'

She arched a perfectly shaped brow. Her mouth had quirked with amusement but there was something in her eyes that negated it; a vulnerability. 'Is that what you call it?'

He shuffled down to kiss her neck. *Dios*, barely minutes since they'd made love and he was hard again. 'What do you prefer to call it?'

'Sex?' From the breathless way she suggested the word he sensed her own arousal sparking back to life.

'I thought the French were a romantic people?'

'We are with people we feel more than hate for.'

'You feel more than hate for me.'

'No, I don't.'

He nipped her shoulder. 'Yes, you do. And what we shared was more than sex.'

'No, it wasn't. And stop telling me what I...' he'd encircled one of her nipples with his tongue '...feel.'

'Ah, I forget you have had *tons* of lovers.'

'I might have exaggerated a little.' Now there was a sensual hitch in her voice.

'When are you going to admit you were a virgin?'

'Never.'

He moved his attention to her other breast, enraptured with its texture, its taste, its weight, the sheer feminine beauty of it... 'You didn't answer my question.'

Her hands found his head, her fingers digging through his hair. 'Which question was that? There have been so many.'

He rested his chin on her nipple to look in her eyes. 'Do you regret us making love...having *sex*?'

The returning stare shone at him. 'I should regret it.'

'But you don't?'

'No.' She wound a lock of his hair in her fingers. 'I don't regret it. It doesn't change how I feel about you or anything else. I still think you're the devil.'

Trailing his tongue up her breast and to her neck, he pressed his mouth back to hers. 'Maybe one day you will discover I am not the devil you think I am,' he said before kissing her deeply.

No more words were spoken between them. Not verbally.

The gecko was back.

Chloe had woken early, much earlier than she

usually liked to wake, and had come to an instant alertness.

That had been a man lying with his head on the pillow next to hers, an arm slung across her midriff. She had moved his arm carefully and sat up to stare at Luis's still-sleeping face.

There had been something surprisingly innocent in his sleeping form, his features smoother except for the now thick stubble around his jawline.

Resisting the urge to press a kiss to the stubbly cheek, she had torn her gaze from him and got out of bed, pausing only to put her thin robe on. Then she had made herself a coffee and slipped through the sliding door and onto the veranda, which was where her two-inch friend had found her.

Of course, it could be a different gecko. Luis's island was full of them. She was sure their parents could differentiate but they all looked the same to her, all except for this one.

This one was cute. It had perched itself on top of the seat next to hers and was staring at her with what she liked to think was interest.

'What do you want, little one?' she asked softly.

'Food? Drink? I would share but I don't think coffee is good for a little thing like you. Are there any bugs you can eat for your breakfast?'

As ridiculous as she knew it was to talk to a reptile, there was a comfort to it. Focusing on the cold-blooded creature stopped her thinking too hard about the warm-blooded creature she'd left sleeping.

This was the first time she'd left the villa's walls since Luis had barged her door open the morning before.

He'd had food brought to them at varying points with jugs of cocktails of varying strengths. She couldn't remember any of it, not what they'd eaten or drunk. The only image with any solidity to it was making love…having sex…with Luis.

The desire that had simmered between them for so long had finally been unleashed and she was in no hurry to tie it back up, not when the things he did to her felt so utterly wonderful.

Luis had taught her things her imagination had never conjured, taught her pleasure that was about so much more than the mechanics of sex.

What had surprised her the most was how fun it had all been. There had been passion—lots of passion—but there had been laughter too. Dirty jokes. A shared bath that had ended with far more water on the floor than in the tub.

She was French, she'd reminded herself many times that day. Taking a lover meant nothing. That her lover was her...fiancé—was that what she was supposed to call the blackmailing, kidnapping devil?—was irrelevant.

But she didn't feel like a kidnap victim. In truth, she'd never felt like his victim. His pawn, yes, that was an apt description but victim, no.

She had known when she'd offered to help her brother that there would be a price to pay in putting herself up against Luis.

A shiver ran up her spine. She shook it off.

Better to have lost her virginity with a man who made her stomach melt with one skim of his finger on her skin than with...

But that was the problem. There never had been anyone else. When she and Luis were done with she still could not envisage herself with anyone else.

She couldn't reconcile her insatiable hunger for him. It was wrong on so many levels that soon she would be joining him in the special level built just for him in Dante's *Inferno*.

The patio door slid open and Luis stepped out onto the veranda, cup of coffee in hand, charcoal boxers slung low over his hips…and nothing else.

Chloe gaped, struck anew at his rugged, masculine beauty.

With the early morning sun beaming down on him he looked like a statue of a Greek god brought to life and filled with bronzed colour, albeit a Greek god with hair sticking up all over the place and eyes puffy from sleep.

For some reason, seeing him like this made her want to cry.

The smile he bestowed her with made her heart double flip on itself.

'You know that talking to yourself is the first sign of madness?' he said casually.

It took a beat for her to get what *he* was talking about.

She grinned, although it was an effort to make her lips and cheeks comply. 'I've been talking to Greta.'

'Greta?'

'Greta the Gecko.' She nodded to the chair Greta was perched on.

Luis took a step towards it and Greta fled.

'You've scared her away,' Chloe chided.

'I have that effect on women,' he teased, taking Greta's vacated seat.

He certainly did, she acknowledged with a painful twist of her heart.

Luis was a man any right-thinking woman would run a mile from.

She had run, as fast as she could.

And then she had drawn him back.

It suddenly struck her that the method she had chosen to get him out of the way for the gala had put her directly in his firing line when there must have been numerous other methods that wouldn't have pointed the finger at her as perpetrator.

But she had *wanted* him to know her part in it. She had imagined his face when he'd worked it all out and taken bitter satisfaction from it while her heart had splintered.

And why had she chosen to make out she was a damsel in distress? Because she had known he was a man who would never let a woman be alone and in potential danger when he could help her.

He'd carried her out of the tree, hadn't he, when he had been only fifteen…?

Luis's fundamental nature was, not exactly good, but selfless. He'd put his own life on the line to help a small child.

Had Benjamin got it all wrong as Luis insisted?

Before she could follow her train of thought any further, Luis put his cup on the table and opened his other hand to reveal a rectangular foil package.

CHAPTER EIGHT

LUIS WATCHED CHLOE'S REACTION, being careful
to keep his own lurching emotions in check.

Her cheeks were stained red. 'Have you been
going through my things?' she croaked.

'No, *bonita*. I saw them on the dining table with
the rest of the contents of your bag. They caught
my eye. You're on the pill?'

He thought of the trio of condoms he'd had
in his wallet, which they'd used up in relatively
short order, and the other ways of making love
they had embraced that hadn't required actual
penetration since.

She stared back at him, the same thoughts obviously going through her mind too because darker
colour flooded her cheeks.

Although incredibly willing, there had been a
shyness about her over all the new things they
had done, a shyness not quite disguised with

laughter and quips. He'd found it utterly beguiling, just as he found most things about her.

When they had run out of condoms and he hadn't wanted to break the headiness of the spell they had created together to return to his villa for more, she hadn't breathed a word that she was already protected.

He hadn't wanted to break the spell until their limbs were so heavy and sated that the only bodily command they could obey was the one demanding sleep. In the back of his mind had been the certainty that the moment he walked out of this villa, what they were sharing would be over.

The chemistry between them had in no way been a precursor to what they would be like together.

Spending the day in bed making love...it had made him forget why he had her there, her conspiracy against him and the consequences he and his brother were living through. It had been passionate and, strangely, fun, a heady combination he had never experienced before.

'I had a bad outbreak of acne when I was nineteen so my doctor put me on the pill to help,' she blurted out, cutting through the increasingly tense silence that had formed between them. 'I stayed on it because I found it helped with the monthly pain.'

Luis dragged a hand through his hair and muttered a curse under his breath, suddenly feeling like a heel.

It had been a reflex action. He'd seen the packet, recognised it, and scooped it up to examine it. It hadn't been a conscious decision to confront her over it. What was there to confront? It was *sensible* for her not to trust him or any other man to keep her safe.

Luis knew his reputation with women wasn't the greatest. There was some truth in his playboy reputation, he had to admit, but it wasn't the whole truth. He'd never hopped from one bed to the next like some of the Lotharios he knew, but didn't see the point in pretending to pine for a relationship that had run its course…although, to call these interludes relationships was pushing it a little.

Marriage or anything remotely long-term had never been on the cards for him. None of the women had wanted to be in a relationship with him, Luis, the man, just with Luis Casillas, child of the murdered Clara Casillas and her killer husband Yuri Abramova, generous host of great parties and generous giver of gifts.

The point was, he told himself firmly, he always used condoms. Always. He didn't care if his lover was on the pill *and* had an IUD fitted, he used condoms, end of discussion.

It must be sleep deprivation that made it feel like a stab in the guts that Chloe didn't trust him to keep her safe.

Their relationship was nothing to do with trust. The sex, great as it was, gave it an added piquancy but that was all.

Chloe owed him nothing but marriage.

'You don't have to explain yourself, *bonita*. I apologise for embarrassing you.'

'You haven't embarrassed me,' she insisted even though her cheeks, flaming all over again, contradicted her statement.

'*Bueno.*'

'No, really, you haven't embarrassed me.' A sudden hint of mischief flashed in her eyes. 'After all, I am a woman of great sexual experience.'

Her obvious and deliberate lie was so outrageous that he burst into laughter.

She caught his gaze and burst out laughing too.

It was only a minor moment but the tightness that had formed in his chest loosened and, with it, the tension between them defused.

She did not owe him a thing more than she had already pledged. Chloe had agreed to marry him. That she was now sharing a bed with him was a delicious bonus.

Very delicious.

Luis settled back in his chair and sipped his coffee, admiring how Chloe could look so fresh and ravishing after such little sleep, slouched back in her chair as she was. She had on only a white robe tied loosely around her waist, the V of it gaping enough for him to see the divine swell of her wonderful breasts.

He exhaled a long sigh. A part of him wanted to press her back on the table and make love to her, the other part content to merely sit there and soak in her rare, unblemished beauty.

His suspicions had been confirmed. He really had been her first.

He'd been as gentle as he could be the first time

he'd possessed her and if she had suffered any pain from it she had covered it well. They had been amazing together.

It struck him then that if he was her first, it stood to reason that one day some other man would be her second.

'Are you comfortable in marrying me knowing it won't last?' he asked curiously.

She arched a brow. 'Are *you?*'

'Very comfortable. Marriage has never been on my agenda.'

'It's never been on mine, either.' Although the fresh, light stain of colour that crawled up her neck made him suspect that there was something there she was keeping from him. 'Marriage is an outdated institution. People make those vows every day without meaning them. At least there's an honesty in the vows we'll make.'

'Are you speaking of your parents' marriage?'

'Their marriage was never honest.' Her eyes held his. 'Did you know your mother and my mother deliberately planned it so they fell pregnant at the same time?'

'That has been alluded to over the years,' he said. He and Javier were only three months older than Benjamin. Whenever his mother had toured, Benjamin and his mother would go with them, Louise as his mother's costume-maker, Benjamin as their playmate.

'My father was, in essence, a sperm donor. My mother married him because she didn't want to be a single mother but she raised Benjamin *as* a single mother. My father had little involvement or say in his upbringing, which was how he liked it. He got the glory of a son without any of the work.'

'I didn't know your father.' He'd been nothing but a name to them. Benjamin had rarely mentioned him.

'Their marriage was all but dead when Maman got broody again.' She rubbed her nose and gave a sad laugh. 'He was ready to leave her but she got him drunk and seduced him. *Et voilà*, nine months later I was born. He left before I was born.'

Luis ran a hand through his hair at this revelation he had known nothing about. 'Your mother told you this?'

'*Non*, my father told me the day before I left his home. He never wanted me and he hated my mother for tricking him into being a sperm donor for a second time.'

He gazed at the beautiful elfin face staring back at him with the merest hint of defiance to counteract the wobble of her chin.

'You learned all this after your mother died?'

She gave a sharp nod.

'That must have been a hard thing to accept.'

She shrugged but her chin wobbled again. 'It explained why he'd never been in my life. I'd only met him three times before Maman died.'

He gave a low whistle. 'Obviously I was aware there wasn't much in the way of involvement from him but I didn't realise it was that bad.'

'It was good,' she insisted. 'My childhood was incredibly happy. He's the one who chose not to be a part of it.'

'So why did you move in with him? Couldn't you have lived with Benjamin?'

'It wasn't allowed. I had only just turned seventeen, I was still at school and still a minor, so that's how it had to be. One parent dies so you move in with the other even if he is a stranger to you. And at the time Benjamin was struggling to cope financially—it wouldn't have been fair to burden him with me too, not then.'

Benjamin had been struggling financially because he'd taken out a huge mortgage to buy the chateau for his mother to end her days in and then neglected his business to care for her in those last days. The savings he'd had to purchase the chateau outright had been given to Luis and Javier for the Tour Mont Blanc land.

Another unintended consequence of that damned contract that Luis was becoming sure would haunt him in the afterlife.

'But you moved in with him eventually, didn't you?' he asked, his brow furrowed. 'I remember visiting the chateau once and you were there. I remember him telling me his fears about you moving to London.'

'I stuck it out with my dad and stepmother until I completed high school then moved in with Benjamin for a while before I moved to London. When I moved back to France after I'd completed my apprenticeship I split my time between his chateau and his apartment in Paris.'

'You never went back to your father's home?'

'*Non.*'

'Did they treat you badly?'

She made a sound like a laugh. It was the most miserable sound Luis had ever heard from her. 'They didn't treat me like anything. They might as well have had a ghost move in for all the attention they paid me. My mother was dead and they couldn't have cared less. They clothed and fed me and made sure I attended school but that was it. They were always out, seeing friends, going on holidays, but they never included me or invited me anywhere with them. I didn't get a single embrace from either of them in the whole year I lived with them. I could understand it from my stepmother but from my father...'

Chloe blinked back the burn of tears.

She would never cry over her father again.

When she'd left her father's home she'd sworn to forget all about him. She'd survived perfectly well for the first seventeen years of her life without him; she didn't need him.

But it still hurt. It really, really hurt.

Whatever the circumstances of her conception, she had been innocent. Benjamin had been innocent. Their father hadn't just walked out on their mother but his ten-year-old son and unborn child too.

The first time he had met his daughter, Chloe had been three years old. It had been another four years before she'd seen him again.

'They didn't want me there,' she explained, trying her hardest to keep her voice factual and moderate. 'I learned when I turned eighteen that my mother had saved all her child support payments from him. It wasn't a fortune but was enough for me to live with Benjamin without being a financial burden.'

'Your father didn't object?'

She gave another miserable laugh. 'He couldn't wait to be rid of me.'

And that was what hurt the most. Deep down Chloe had wanted him to object. She'd wanted him to raise himself up and insist on being her father. She'd wanted to be important to him. She'd wanted him to love her but he didn't. He never had and never would.

She had never spoken about any of this before. Benjamin knew she'd had a hard time living with their father but she'd never confided the depth of her misery there or the enormous one-sided argument she and her father had had, scared she would come across as a spoilt, needy brat. Her stepmother, in a rare moment of interaction with Chloe, had called her exactly that.

It had been a one-sided argument because it had essentially consisted of Chloe having a complete breakdown. She had screamed at her father, all her misery and pain pouring out of her in an emotional tirade that had been met by her father's cold retelling of the past and her stepmother's cruel words.

The closest she had come to that feeling of betrayal and helplessness and that total loss of emotional control was with the man whose arms she had found such pleasure in.

She hadn't seen her father since the day she'd left.

A buzzing sound rang out.

'That will be our breakfast.' Luis jumped to his feet, grateful for the disturbance.

After defusing the tension between them things had suddenly become extremely weighty.

He admired Chloe's spirit, her beauty, her feistiness...

Her vulnerability was not something he liked

to see and there had been more than a flash of it then as she'd narrated a part of her life he'd only known the basics of.

Dios, her father's treatment of his child had been as deplorable as his father's, even if their methods of abuse had differed. Chloe's father had abused her with his indifference. Luis's father had abused him with his hands.

'Stay there. I'll let them in.'

Pulling a pair of shorts on first, he opened the door to find Sara and Jalen. The little boy took one look at him and hid behind his mother.

Sara rolled her tired eyes and said apologetically. 'He was hoping to see Chloe. My son has taken quite a shine to her.'

Remembering the hip-hop dancing the boy had been doing with her, Luis quite understood why.

'I will tell her you were asking for her,' he said to the boy pretending to be invisible behind his mother's legs, before taking the breakfast tray from Sara's hands.

At some point soon he would have to employ more staff for the island. Marietta hadn't been to the island in the three years before she'd sold it to him and had let all the other permanent staff go.

Sara had proved herself to be an excellent cook but she had a hundred other jobs to get on with.

He carried the tray out onto the veranda and set it on the table.

Chloe gave him a small smile.

As she helped herself to toast, he said, 'Your boyfriend was asking after you.'

Her brow furrowed in confusion. 'What?'

'The caretakers' boy.'

He did not want to go back to tales of her childhood. Listening had had the effect of a hook being wound around his stomach.

His diversion did the trick.

'Jalen?' Her face lit up. 'Oh, he's a sweet little thing.'

'He hides or runs away whenever he sees me.'

She shrugged with bemusement. 'You're three times the size of him. To his eyes you're a big scary giant.'

'You think?'

'He told me that himself.'

'It's not men in particular that he's fearful of?'

'No—why do you ask?'

'I keep thinking of his reaction when his father

called him over the day we got here. He looked terrified.'

Chloe grinned. 'That's because his father had expressly forbidden him from speaking to us.'

'Why would he do that?'

'You're the new boss. They don't know you and they don't know how tolerant you are to children. They're worried for their jobs. They're scared that if you think Jalen is a nuisance you will re-place them with childless caretakers.'

'Jalen told you all this?'

'He's a chatterbox without a filter.' Her pretty white teeth flashed at him again. 'I can under-stand why they're scared of him talking to you.'

'They have nothing to worry about. I appreciate that this is their home…you are sure that that's the only reason Jalen was afraid of his father?'

Her eyes narrowed slightly as she tilted her head. 'He wasn't afraid of his father, he was afraid of the telling-off he knew he would get from him.'

He nodded slowly. It was the way Jalen had hung his head while speaking to his father that had sent the alarm bells ringing in him. It had taken him back thirty years to how he would stand when summoned to see his father.

'I suppose all children are afraid of their father some of the time.' Luis had been one of the unlucky ones who had been afraid of his father all of the time. The only times he'd ever fully relaxed as a child was when he and Javier had gone on tour with their mother without him.

Chloe was watching him closely. He could see the questions swirling in her head, her curiosity piqued.

The tension that had filled him when he'd discovered her contraceptive pill packet and her matter-of-fact explanation on her relationship with her father crowded back into him.

He got back to his feet and leaned over to place a hard, hungry kiss to her mouth. 'I'm going to my villa. I'll be back in five,' he murmured into the silkiness of her hair before kissing her again.

When he broke away there was a dazed look in her eyes, her questions successfully driven away.

He returned to her in four minutes with his pockets stuffed with condoms and carried her to the bedroom.

CHAPTER NINE

CHLOE FINISHED HER lunch with Jalen on the beach then headed to the main villa where Luis had spent the morning working.

Butterflies rampaged through her belly, the product, she told herself, of nerves that they were going to sign their pre-nuptial agreement, not excitement at seeing him again. That was a ludicrous notion. He'd only left her bed four hours ago.

But it frightened her how much she had missed him in those four hours apart.

No, she told herself firmly, it was the sex she missed. Two days of doing nothing but making love was bound to affect her and, as a lover, although she had no one to compare him to, Luis was amazing. They were amazing together. So long as they kept things physical then everything was fine.

She still struggled to understand why she had

divulged her relationship with her father to him. She'd crossed an invisible line there and had only just stopped herself from crossing it again when they had been talking about Jalen.

There had been an undercurrent running behind Luis's questions about the boy, and she'd recalled the fleeting concern she'd seen on his face when Jalen had been scolded by his father.

Scared of being alone with her thoughts, she had sought Jalen out, assuring Sara repeatedly that he was no bother at all. She liked the little boy's company. There was no artifice to him, everything laid out in that innocent way only a child could manage.

Sara opened the door with a welcoming smile and invited her to wait in one of the living rooms while she let Luis know she was there.

The living room in question was an enormous elegant space with a distinctly feminine touch to it. Chloe stared at all the clutter and boxes filling it with awed disbelief. How did any one person accumulate so much *stuff*?

A huge, elaborately framed portrait at the front of a stack of frames resting against the wall caught Chloe's attention. It showed a young, strangely old-fashioned beautiful woman with thick curly black hair, posing elegantly with an enigmatic smile.

'I'm sorry about the mess,' Sara said, slipping back into the room. 'We are packing up Marietta's things to get them shipped to her. It's taking us a lot longer than we thought it would.'

Chloe smiled then pointed at the portrait. 'Is that Marietta?' The armchair the sitter had posed in was in the corner of the room.

'It is.'

Something sharp stabbed into Chloe's heart. So this was the woman who had sold her yacht and her island to Luis in the space of days.

Her stomach curdled again to imagine the *incentives* Luis must have brought to the table to convince her so quickly.

The ghost of Marietta had haunted her since she had arrived at this beautiful island, a phantom reminder that, to Luis, women were disposable.

'She was only eighteen when this was painted,' Sara explained. 'Her father had it done to celebrate her coming of age.'

'He must adore her,' she said, unable to contain her wistfulness.

Chloe had been living with her father on her eighteenth birthday and he'd still managed to forget it. The huge row that had exploded between them the day before she had moved out of his emotionally cold, horrible house had resulted in Chloe being struck from his address book permanently. She doubted he knew she now lived in Madrid.

Sara laughed. 'I don't know about that. It was the done thing with the gentry in those days.'

'What do you mean?'

'That portrait is over seventy years old.'

Chloe's jaw dropped. 'Seriously?'

'Marietta's going to be ninety on her next birthday.'

She stepped over to look at the portrait in more detail and crouched down. Close up it was even more majestic.

Footsteps sounded behind her.

'It's incredible to think this is seventy years old,' she murmured. 'It's in remarkable condition, and the detail…'

'It's something special, yes?'

Chloe almost fell backwards onto her bottom. She hadn't heard Luis enter the room, had thought Sara had come to stand behind her.

He held out a hand to her.

Her legs wobbling in protest at her crouching position, she grabbed onto it and let him help her up.

'Thank you,' she murmured, disconcerted to find her heart racing.

His eyes sparkled. 'Pleasure.'

She felt more unsettled than ever. Her insides were a cauldron bubbling with a thousand differing emotions, all of which boiled for him.

But she would not show it. She would never let Luis know how easily and seamlessly he had burrowed under her skin.

Smiling broadly, she pulled out the contract she'd shoved into the back pocket of her shorts. 'Shall we get this signed?'

Sara and her husband Rodrigo were going to act as their witnesses.

'You are happy with the terms?'

'What terms?' she snorted. There had been only one; the one forbidding her from speaking publicly about any part of their relationship. She would be gagged for ever from speaking about Luis in any shape or form.

It was a term she could live with.

She would never do anything to fuel the poison out there about him.

At some point she would need to speak to her brother and warn him. It would have to be done before she and Luis exchanged their vows. How Benjamin would take it she couldn't begin to predict. Her brother's hatred of both Casillas brothers ran so deep she had no way of knowing if he would listen to reason.

Surely he wouldn't have wanted all this poison for them?

But her brother was wounded. Their betrayal had cut him so deeply that his instinct had been to lash out. Chloe understood that because it had been the same for her.

Had Luis been right when he'd accused her of using it as an excuse to run away from him?

'Before we sign, let me give you a tour of the house,' he said, cutting into her thoughts. 'I need a fresh pair of eyes to help me decide how to redecorate this place.'

'Isn't that what interior designers are for?'

'And I will employ one but right now it's your opinion I'm interested in.'

Curiosity piqued, Chloe let herself be guided through the magnificent villa that was more than a match in size for her brother's chateau. But where Benjamin's chateau was decorated and maintained to the highest possible standard, the deeper into the villa she went, the more its neglect shone through.

'Marietta inherited it from her father,' Luis explained as he took her into the library. 'It had been in the family for generations and Marietta was the end of the line.'

'Did she not have children?'

'No. She never married either. She was a socialite who preferred life on the bigger islands and in Manhattan. She used this island as her personal holiday home for her and her closest friends but she never liked living here. She found it too isolating.'

'Is that why she was happy to sell it to you?'

'She hasn't set foot on the island in three years. She lives permanently in Manhattan now. I made her an outrageous offer for the island and the yacht and she accepted on the spot. She'd kept it for so long only out of an old sense of duty. The yacht was just one of her many toys she bored of playing with.'

Chloe looked up at the faded wallpaper fraying away from the ceiling.

To think she had assumed he'd seduced Marietta into selling up...

For some reason to know she had been way off the mark made her feel lighter inside.

A burst of laughter flew from her mouth. 'I still can't believe you would spend that much money just to kidnap me.'

'To make money you have to spend money. In this case, to preserve my fortune and salvage my reputation, I had to spend a good sum. It's money well spent. And I got a yacht and an island out of it,' he added with a grin before pulling her in for one of the heady kisses she was becoming addicted to. 'I'm already thinking ahead to the parties I will host here once I've renovated the place and had a runway put in.'

She hooked her arms around his neck and gazed into his eyes. Luis had shaved since he'd left her bed. The scent of his fresh cologne danced into her senses in the dreamiest of fashions. 'Won't having a runway ruin what makes the island so special?'

'I'll keep the runway small and discreet. There won't be any jets landing here.'

'Good.'

He grinned. 'You should come to one of my parties. You can do the hip-hop dancing I saw you doing on the beach.'

'By the time you've renovated the house and sorted out a runway, you and I will be long over,' she pointed out.

Instead of the joy she expected to flush through her at the thought of the day her life became her own again, her stomach plummeted.

The gleam in his eyes made the slightest of dims before his grin regained full wattage and he tugged her arms away from his neck.

Keeping a firm hold of her hand, he led her up the winding staircase that creaked on every tread. 'You should still come. Your hip-hop dancing is very entertaining.'

She forced a laugh.

She much preferred it when they were making love and she could concentrate on the physical side of their relationship, because that was all their relationship would ever amount to and there was no point in allowing the old dreams she'd once had for him rear their head again. She wasn't a teenager any more. She'd seen enough of life to know dreams did not come true.

'I've never had much rhythm,' she told him.

'I remember when you were small. You were always wearing a tutu.'

'That's when I was young. I grew up in a house that my brother called a shrine to dance. My mother was crazy about it and had me in dance classes when I was three.'

'Did you not enjoy it?'

She hesitated before admitting, 'My dream was to dance like your mother.'

The shrine to ballet that had been her childhood home should really have been called a shrine to Clara Casillas. Pictures of her in dance had framed all the walls, along with tour posters and pictures of the two women, Clara and Chloe's mother, Louise, together. The latter had been Chloe's favourite pictures. Her absolute favourite had been one taken in Clara's dressing room in New York. Clara had been dressed in a red embellished costume, Chloe's mother on her knees making adjustments to the hem. In the background, sitting squashed together cross-legged under Clara's dressing table were three small boys all with sulky faces. Benjamin, Luis and Javier. That picture had made her smile for so many different reasons.

When their mother had died, Chloe and Benjamin had gone through all her things together. He had been happy for Chloe to have the ballet memorabilia, all except for that one picture. He'd explained that it had been taken minutes after he and the Casillas twins had been scolded for trying to set off the theatre's fire alarm. Their mothers had made them sit in silence for ten minutes, threatening the withdrawal of the promised after-show pizza for non-compliance.

Her eyes met Luis's, the middle child in that long-ago picture. A fleeting sadness passed between them that pierced straight into her heart.

'What stopped you pursuing ballet?' he asked after a sharp inhalation.

'I told you, my lack of rhythm.' Then she sighed. 'To be truthful, I lived in denial for many years. I always hoped that one day the rhythm would find me and I would turn from the ugly duckling of dance to the swan but it wasn't to be.'

'When did you give it up?'

'When I was thirteen and my breasts exploded from molehills to mountains. Have you seen a ballerina with large breasts? They don't exist, do they? I had so little talent that no one bothered suggesting breast reduction surgery for me. I used that as the excuse for giving it up but, really, everyone who had ever seen me dance knew the reason was simply that I wasn't good enough.'

'I'm sorry you had to give up your dream.'

She shrugged. 'There are worse dreams to give up…'

Like the dream of having a father who actually wanted to be a father. Living under his roof for barely a year had been the final proof that dreams really did not come true no matter how hard she wished them.

Her ballet dream had always been more of a wispy cloud than anything concrete.

Her dreams of a miracle cure suddenly appearing for her mother… Chloe had seen the cancer ravaging her mother with her own eyes and known that to focus on a cure when the present was all she had left with her would ruin the remaining time they had together. But that dream had still been there, buried deep, getting her through the nights until time had finally run out.

She'd never realised how concrete her dream of wanting her father to *be* her father had been until she'd learned that it was never going to come true. That was a dream that couldn't come true not through a lack of talent or a lack of a medical cure but because *he* didn't want it to happen.

Dreams did not come true. Chloe would never be Clara Casillas. Her mother had died. Her father would never love her. And Luis would never...

Luis would never what? Love her either?

She didn't *want* his love. All she wanted from him was her freedom.

'And I always liked watching Maman create costumes,' she continued, blinking back the sting of hot tears that had sneaked up on her without warning. 'It turned out that costume-making was a talent I did have and the good thing about it is I don't have to watch what I eat or exercise for a hundred hours a day.'

She'd realised in the first week of her apprenticeship at the London ballet company that she would not have made it as a professional ballet dancer even if she'd had the talent. To reach the top as a ballet dancer required self-discipline and a *lot* of sacrifice. She'd had the dream but it had never been matched by the needed hunger.

She liked the niche she'd carved as a costume maker, liked that she'd followed her mother's footsteps, liked the camaraderie and the creativity. She had the best job in the world...

Anger and pride had had her denying to Luis that she cared about losing her career and in that heated moment on his yacht she had meant it. But now, with tempers cooled, it chilled her skin to think how perilously close she had come to throwing it all away.

She had to hope that when this was all over with Luis she would find another ballet company to take her on.

'It does take dedication to reach the top,' he agreed, opening another door. As with all the other doors he'd opened, Chloe took only a cursory look at the room behind it, her attention on their conversation.

'Did you ever dance?' she asked. Luis was the son of two professional dancers. The masculinity issue that prevented many boys from trying ballet would not have applied in his household.

'Me? *Dios*, no. My mother tried to encourage us but neither of us had the slightest interest in it. We just wanted to play.'

She hesitated before asking, 'What about your father?'

A hardness crept into his voice. 'What about him?'

'Did he not encourage you and Javier to follow in his footsteps?'

'Not that I remember.' He opened another door and smoothly changed the subject. 'This was Marietta's bedroom. I'm debating whether to turn it into my own bedroom. What do you think?'

She thought that she needed to respect his reluctance to speak about his father but that undercurrent was there again and, against her better judgement, she said, 'What was your father like?'

'You know what he was like. The world knows what he was like.'

'If I ever met him as a toddler I don't remember it. Benjamin never spoke of him. I know what I've read about him but I would think only a very small part of it is based on truth.'

'No, you will find the majority of it is based on truth. I hated him.'

At the widening of her eyes, Luis took a deep breath, fighting for air in his closed-up lungs.

'Was he always violent towards your mother?' she whispered.

'As far as I know—and your mother confirmed this to me—my father was never physically violent to my mother until the night he killed her.' He relayed this matter-of-factly, hiding the manic thrumming of his heart that even the mildest of allusions to that night always broke out in him. 'I took the brunt of his anger.'

'In what way?'

'In the way that involved belts across naked backsides. It was a form of corporal punishment that was accepted in those days.'

'Just you?'

He nodded curtly. 'He never touched Javier. When we got into trouble together the blame would be put on my shoulders.'

'Even if Javier was at fault?'

'In fairness to Javier, he rarely instigated any trouble. I was the ringleader. I was drawn to trouble like a magnet. When your brother toured with us he was a far more willing accomplice than Javier.' He took another long breath and put a hand to the flaking doorframe, ready to put a stop to this conversation immediately. Instead, he found himself saying, 'Our father was a bitter man. You know he defected from the Soviet Union in the early seventies?'

She nodded, wide-eyed.

'He was a star to the western world back then, another Nureyev. When he met my mother in London she was an up-and-coming ingénue fifteen years his junior. Her star was not supposed to eclipse his but eventually it did and he hated her for it. Our mother carried us twins and returned to the stage stronger than ever. As her star rose his faded. He was always a drinker and prone to outbursts of temper but when he started fighting choreographers and fellow cast members, he no longer had the star power for companies to turn a blind eye. Work dried up. His resentment towards my mother grew. There were months when we wouldn't see anything of him—those were the best times—then he would reappear on the scene and act as if he had never been away.'

'Didn't your mother mind?'

He shook his head as bile curdled up his throat. 'Theirs was a strange relationship. The power balance always tilted from one to the other. They both had lovers. They both flaunted it. But then my father found the young lovers he wanted no longer wanted him; and why would they? He was a drunken mess. He couldn't touch my mother so he took his anger out on me.'

'Didn't she stop him?'

'He was my father. To her mind it was his duty to punish me when it was deserved. She was no disciplinarian herself.' He felt the smallest of smiles break over skin that had become like marble to remember his mother trying to hide her amusement at their japes by putting on her 'stern' face. 'She never raised a finger to us. If my father's punishments went too far she would cup my cheeks and tell me to smile through the pain.'

He heard Chloe suck in a breath.

'My mother understood corporal punishment,' he said, compelled to defend the mother he had loved. 'Her own parents would often use it to punish her. To my mother it was normal and, though she couldn't bring herself to physically punish us herself, she cited it as toughening her up and giving her the tools she needed to succeed in such a competitive world. Her ballet training had taught her to smile through the pain and she wanted me to have that resilience too.'

There was a long period of silence before she asked, 'Why do you think he chose to punish only you?'

'He never liked me. There was something in me that pushed his buttons; I don't know what it was. He adored Javier.'

'That must have been hard.'

'Harder for Javier,' he dismissed. 'It hurt him to see *me* be hurt. We are not identical but we *are* twins and we've had each other's back our entire lives. It is a bond that no one can come between. He suffered in his own way too—our mother loved us both but she doted on me. That was hard on him. He always tried to protect me. He was always trying to save me from the worst of my behaviour because he could always see what the consequences would be.'

'Couldn't you see them?'

'I could but I didn't care.' Just as he'd seen that the consequences of keeping silent about the profit share with Benjamin could be dire but had kept his mouth shut through the years rather than rock a friendship that had meant so much to him.

His relationship with his brother was like a rock, solid and impenetrable. His friendship with Benjamin, which had been stronger than Javier's and Benjamin's, had had the fun element to it. They had broken the rules together, Javier tagging along not to join in with the rule-breaking but to try and stop them going too far.

Benjamin had been his closest friend. He grieved the end of their friendship but in life you had to look forward. Always look forward. Never let the past hook you back.

But the past was hooking him back. He could feel its weight clasped around his stomach, the tentacles digging in tighter and tighter with each hour that passed.

'Maybe it was because you look so much like your mother,' she said softly.

'What was?'

'Your father... Javier looks so much like him whereas you resemble your mother. Maybe he preferred Javier because he thought of him as a miniature version of himself.'

Her words were a variant of Javier's attempts to placate him over their father's cruelty.

Luis moved his hand away from the frame to run it through his hair then caught the flakes of paint on his palm and wiped it on his shorts instead.

The main house needed to be bulldozed and started again from the foundations upwards, he thought moodily.

Unfortunately he had made a promise to Marietta that he would keep the actual structure intact.

He looked back at Chloe, took in the compassion ringing from those beautiful eyes and suppressed a shudder.

Her experiences, different from his as they were, were similar enough that she would have an inkling of what he had felt when growing up.

He needed to keep the structure of their relationship intact too. A marriage that lasted long enough to kill the nastiness circulating about him and his brother. They would have fun and enjoy the time they had together but there would be no bonds between them other than the bonds made in the bedroom.

'No,' he denied with more ice than she deserved. 'It was nothing to do with any physical resemblance. My father disliked me because there was nothing in me for him to like.'

At the parting of her lips, he pressed a finger to them. 'Enough about my father. He's dead. The past is over.' And why he was rehashing long-past deeds with Chloe was beyond his comprehension. His past had nothing to do with their marriage. 'The future's what matters now. And now I would like your honest opinion about this room as I am thinking of making it my bedroom.'

Only his.

As she had rightly said, he and Chloe would be long over when this house was fit for purpose.

He would be the one to pull the trigger to topple the structures holding them together.

CHAPTER TEN

'ARE YOU GOING to join me?' Luis cajoled from the side of the pool.

Chloe, who'd been admiring his strong, powerful strokes from the safety of her sun lounger, shook her head.

Another day in paradise…

After spending the entire morning in bed making love, Luis had suddenly declared himself in need of exercise.

She'd raised a disbelieving eyebrow at that, which had made him laugh and plant an enormous kiss on her mouth. Then he'd strode naked from the bed, strolled through the villa and down to the bottom of the garden and dived straight into the swimming pool, still unashamedly naked.

And with that glorious body, why should he be ashamed? she'd thought dreamily as she'd spied on him from the bedroom window before slipping a bikini on and moving outside for a better view. Luis was a man made for a physical life and the more time he spent showing that physical prowess off in the most physical way with her, the better...

Her increasingly erotic thoughts about him were cut short when Luis hauled himself out of the water and scooped her into his arms.

'Into the water with you,' he said with a grin as he carried her effortlessly to the water's edge despite water dripping off him.

'Put me down,' she squealed, panic setting in instantaneously as she threw her arms around his neck and clung on tightly.

He held her over the water. 'Scared of getting your hair wet?' he teased.

'I can't swim!'

He took an immediate step back and stared down at her with a combination of bemusement and concern. 'Are you serious?'

'Yes!' she yelled. 'Now, put me down!'

Carrying her back to the sun lounger, he gently deposited her on it then grabbed the towel she'd brought down for him and rubbed it through his hair.

'You really can't swim?'

She rolled her eyes. 'I really cannot swim.'

'Why not?'

'Because I hate getting my hair wet.'

He wiped his hand over the droplets of water shining on his chest and flicked it at her hair.

'Behave.'

He laughed and helped himself to a glass of the orange juice Chloe had also brought out. He drained it, wrapped the towel around his waist and sat next to her.

'You're not vain enough to care about your hair getting wet,' he observed with a grin.

She grinned back at him. 'Benjamin tried to teach me when I was little but I hated the shock of the cold water and refused to go any deeper than my thighs.'

'So you never learned?'

'I hate the cold. And I was a stubborn thing.'

'Some would say you still are.'

She mock-glowered at him and, to better show her disdain, swung her legs round to rest on his wonderful, muscular thighs.

He shook his head mockingly and rubbed a hand on her calf. 'The water here is the perfect temperature. I could teach you.'

She made a non-committal grunt. Chloe had managed perfectly well without swimming and didn't see that she'd missed out on anything by preferring to be on land.

'It's better to be able to swim,' he pointed out. 'You never know when it will come useful.'

'Says the man who was probably born able to swim like a world champion.' His prowess in the water was a thing of wonder.

Now he was the one to make a grunt-like noise. 'Hardly. I didn't learn until I was eight.'

'That's late, isn't it? Benjamin had given up on teaching me by then.'

'I learned on our only family sunshine holiday. Our father decided he was the man to teach us.'

The tone of his voice sent a chill up her spine.

The easy playfulness between them seemed to hover on a pair of scales between them as Chloe weighed up whether to ask anything about it.

Would this be a rare happy childhood tale of his?

It pained her to think that unlikely.

So she went with the most neutral question she could think of. 'Did you pick it up easily?'

'No. Javier did, but like you I was a stubborn thing and did everything wrong.'

'On purpose?'

He nodded. 'One day my father got so angry with me for not trying, he said that in the morning he would throw me in the deep end and it would be up to me to sink or swim.'

Nausea creeping through her, Chloe shifted forward so her arched thighs were pressed against his and stroked his damp arm.

'You believed him,' she whispered, resting her chin on his shoulder. She did not doubt for a second eight-year-old Luis had believed his father would let him drown.

His jaw clenched. 'Javier believed it too. He dragged me to the beach with him—we'd found a cove near the resort that was really secluded and calm—and made me learn.'

'You were eight?' she clarified, stunned to think of two such small boys being allowed to go off on their own.

'It was safe,' he insisted. 'The cove was next to the resort. My parents were having one of their good spells and had gone off for what they called a siesta. We had free rein.'

Chloe knew better than to comment on this, did nothing but continue stroking his arm, making her way down to the palm of his hand and tracing circles around it.

'Javier took me out into the sea and made me lie on my back while he held an arm under me to keep me afloat. He kept telling me that if I could float I would never drown. Chloe... I cannot tell you how scared he was, much more than I. He was crying and begging me to trust him. And I did trust him. He was my twin. Who else in the world could I trust more than the boy who was always trying to save me from myself?'

Chloe closed her eyes, trying hard not to allow sympathy into her heart for the small boy Javier would have been, the boy terrified his father would let his beloved twin drown.

'You floated,' she said softly.

'*Sí.* I floated for my brother's sake. By the end of the holiday we were racing each other in the water.'

'How did your father react when you floated?'

'He didn't do it. I don't know if it was a burst of his meagre conscience or if he forgot but he never did throw me in.'

'I'm glad.'

'So was I.' He took a deep breath then carefully moved her legs from over his thighs and got to his feet.

When he looked at her she could virtually see the shutters that had come down in his eyes.

It was the same look as when he'd told her about his father's abuse. End of discussion.

After the strangest pause where he gazed at her as if seeing her for the first time, he blinked.

The shutters had gone and now he stared at her with that hungry look she knew so well.

He grinned widely and held his hand out to her. 'Come, *bonita*. If you won't get your hair wet in the pool with me then you can get wet in the shower.'

Her heart hurting for him, she let him help her to her feet then, when she was upright, wound her arms around his neck and kissed him deeply.

His fingers speared her hair as he kissed her back, his arousal undeniable despite the thick cotton towel draped around his waist.

How badly she wished she could kiss away his past and drive out the pain she knew on an instinctive level still haunted him.

But then, when he lifted her into his arms and carried her back into the villa, the moment overtook her and all thoughts were driven from her mind as she revelled in the heady pleasure they had found together.

Chloe sat on the beach digging her toes into the soft sand and stared up at the sky. There was no moon that night and the stars were in abundance, twinkling down on her like tiny dazzling jewels.

She had been unable to fall asleep. Her mind was filled with too much for it to switch off.

Her resolve over Luis was made of the same fine sand as this warm beach. She could laugh at her weakness but it frightened her too much to be funny.

In two days she would marry him.

She had lain in the bed with him breathing deeply and rhythmically beside her, her lungs getting tighter and tighter until she couldn't draw air any more.

There was a turbulence in her stomach that had grown stronger with each passing hour spent with him.

She spent *all* her time with him, laughing and

making love. She would gaze into his hazel eyes and feel all the breath leave her in a soar.

And then she would recall their conversations about his childhood and her chest would cramp so tightly she couldn't breathe the air back in.

His childhood had been more violent and tempestuous than she could have imagined. The old stories about his violent father that she'd assumed had been embellished by an insatiable media had, if anything, been underplayed.

He'd come so far, both he and Javier. What they had lived through in their formative years could have destroyed lesser men. Not them. Not Luis.

And then he had shut her out. It had almost been a physical act; a blink of the eye and then shutters appeared in them. She understood it was his way of telling her, without words, to back off, to keep things between them on the loose footing they had agreed on, his way of telling her not to get too close.

There was a reason Luis had reached the age of thirty-five without a single long-term relationship under his belt and she strongly suspected it had its roots in his relationship with his father.

She shouldn't *need* telling. She didn't want their

marriage to be anything other than temporary either and had no clue as to why that turbulence in her stomach felt strong enough to dislodge her heart.

This craving for him, which had grown so much more than physical, had to stop.

'Chloe?'

She turned her head to see Luis emerge from between the palm trees lining this stretch of beach.

'Hi,' she said softly, her pulse surging just to see his silhouette.

He walked to her wearing nothing but a pair of navy shorts and his deck shoes. 'I wondered where you'd got to.'

'I couldn't sleep,' she confessed.

'You should have woken me. Are you okay?'

Her heart twisted to hear the concern in his voice. In his own way, he did care about her.

She nodded. 'I just needed some air.'

He sat down beside her and stretched his long legs out. 'Something on your mind?'

She gave a hollow laugh. 'Right now it feels as if I have the whole world on my mind.'

Silence bloomed between them and then

stretched, a tension in it that she soon found herself desperate to break.

'I keep thinking back to our childhoods,' she said, speaking without really thinking of what she was going to say, just aware that all the stuff that had accumulated in her head as Marietta's possessions had accumulated in the main house needed an outlet. 'Do you remember my mother's funeral? You found me crying and you comforted me. You let me cry in your arms and said things that really resonated and gave me the courage to hope that one day the pain would become bearable. You understood what I was going through. I always remembered that. I carried your words with me for so long… When Benjamin told me about the profit terms with Tour Mont Blanc I felt betrayed, not just for him but for myself and our mother too. I'd been with Benjamin at the hospital the day you made that call to him asking for the money. We'd been told barely an hour before that our mother was dying. I remember him telling you the news. I was holding his hand.'

She felt his eyes burn into her but kept her gaze out on the still sea, black and sparkling under the night sky.

Luis's heart had clenched itself into a fist.

He'd awoken alone in the bed to find Chloe missing. Intellectually he'd known she wouldn't have gone far but there had been a punch of nausea to see the indentation of her head on the pillow.

The hook that had wrapped around his stomach was now so tight it threatened to cut off his blood flow.

If not for the starkness in the way she'd spoken, he would drag her back to bed and distract her in the only way he knew how.

'Being told about your mother's diagnosis is why I have little memory of what occurred the rest of that day,' he said, recalling how Benjamin's news had lanced him.

The Guillem siblings hadn't been the only ones hoping for a miracle.

'Javier and I were fighting to save our business. To then hear your mother's condition was terminal... Chloe, it cut me to pieces.'

'Really?'

The simple hope that rang from her voice sliced through Luis as if it had a blade attached.

'When we went to Benjamin's apartment to

sign it that night I barely gave the contract a second thought. I thought Javier had told him we wanted to renegotiate the terms…'

'But he hadn't.'

He breathed heavily. No. His brother hadn't done. For seven years Luis had believed it to be an oversight on his brother's part but now, as he relived that time in full, he had to wonder…

'Our lawyer and his paralegal came with us to witness it. The contracts were laid out on Benjamin's dining table. He wanted to get it signed and done with. Neither Javier nor I had any way of knowing he hadn't read it. We all signed it, Benjamin transferred the money, Javier and the lawyers left, then Benjamin and I got drunk together.'

'Didn't Javier stay with you?'

'Someone had to finalise the deal with the seller and that someone was Javier. Besides, he doesn't drink.'

His brother had never drunk alcohol. The healthy hell-raising that was a rite of passage for most young men had been left to Luis and Benjamin.

'I drowned my sorrows with your brother because, *bonita*, your mother had been a part of my life from when I was in the womb.' He breathed the salt air in deeply as even older memories hit him in a wave. 'Did you know I was named after her?'

'Non!' she gasped, her head turning to face him. 'You were named after my mother? No one ever told me that.'

He smiled to see how wide her eyes had gone with her disbelief. 'I always felt a bond with her because of it. I will never forget the way she broke the news of my mother's death to us and the kindness and love she showed us that night. My grandparents took good care of us when we became their wards but they were old and would never talk about my mother. They found it too painful.'

The loss of their only child had devastated his grandparents, who had been in their forties and resigned to a childless life when they had un-expectedly conceived Luis and Javier's mother. When they had taken their twin grandsons into their home they had been in their seventies, old-fashioned and set in their ways and unprepared for the mayhem bereaved teenage boys would bring to their orderly lives. When they had tried to discipline Luis in the manner they had disciplined their daughter all those decades before, he'd stood his ground and refused to accept it.

He'd vowed on the death of his mother that he would never again be a whipping boy for anyone. He would never let another person raise a hand to him or look at him with the contempt he'd always seen ringing from his father's eyes.

In Louise Guillem's home Luis had found a modicum of peace. The Guillems' suburban house was near to the Parisian apartment he and Javier had called home with their parents until their lives had been destroyed. Being under Louise's roof with his brother and his best friend, speaking the language that had come more naturally to him than his own had been the only light he had found in those years.

'Your mother found it painful to talk about her too but she was always willing. She kept my mother's memory alive for me. She became the surrogate parent my grandparents weren't capable of being. Carrying her coffin was one of the hardest things I have ever done. Saying goodbye to her was like saying goodbye to my mother all over again.'

A tear glistened on her cheek. She wiped it away and gave a deep sigh. 'I'm glad you loved her. She loved you and Javier very much.' She wiped another spilling tear. 'Can I ask you one more question?'

How could he refuse? 'Anything.'

'Did you ever see your father again, after…?'

After he'd killed Luis's mother.

'Never. I never visited him in prison and I never visited him on his deathbed.'

Their father successfully pleaded diminished responsibility and got convicted of manslaughter. He served only ten years of his sentence, nothing for extinguishing such a precious life.

It had felt fitting that he should die of pancreatic cancer less than a year after his release, alone and unloved.

Only as the years had gone by had regrets started to creep in.

'Do you regret not seeing him?'

Her question was astute.

'My mother has been dead for over twenty years and I still miss her. My father has been dead for half that and I have never missed him but now I wish I had accepted the visiting orders he sent me from prison and taken the opportunity to look him in the eye and ask him how he could have done what he did.'

Her voice was small. 'He did want to see you, then?'

He sighed heavily. 'Yes. He asked for me in the hospice too. He died a very lonely man.'

He pressed his head to hers.

There didn't seem any more need for words. In their own wildly differing ways each had suffered at the hands of their fathers. And in their own way each still suffered at them, Chloe with the indifference she lived with each day, he with the legacy of his mother's murder, a story that would not be extinguished.

Another tear rolled down her cheek. She brushed it with her thumb before lying down on the sand. 'I am so sorry, Luis.'

'Sorry for what?'

'For conspiring with Benjamin against you. I should have known it had never been a deliberate act on your part...'

He wished he could say the same for his brother.

'Hush.' Laying himself down next to her, he gently took her chin and turned her face to look at him. 'Your brother had good reason to think we ripped him off. I regret not handling it better when he confronted us about it but what's done is done. All we can do is put things right for the future.'

'But we have caused such damage, and after everything you've already...'

He put his lips to hers and slid a hand down the curve of her neck. 'Damage our marriage will repair.'

She burrowed her fingers into his hair and gazed intently at him.

The lights from the stars glittered from her tear-filled eyes, desire mingling with her pain, all there ringing at him. Another solitary drop spilled down her cheek.

Suddenly unable to bear looking into those depths any longer, he kissed the tear away then plundered that beautiful mouth with his own, taking her pain away the only way he knew how.

Her response was as passionate as it always was, their desire for each other a simmering flame that only needed the slightest coaxing to bring fully to life.

It was so easy to lose himself in her softness and her passion. There was such openness in her lovemaking; no pretence, no artifice, nothing hidden, just a celebration of the joy their lovemaking evoked, there in her every touch and moan.

As he pulled her dress off and kissed the breasts he just could not get enough of, it came to him that he'd changed as a lover. The pleasure he gave Chloe was far more intoxicating than the great pleasure she gave him, never an exercise in ticking boxes until the time was right for him to take his pleasure but an erotic, heady experience all of its own.

When it came to giving pleasure there was nothing he would not do for her.

And it was the same for her too.

Chloe was the most unselfish lover he could have dreamed of.

Trailing his tongue down her soft belly to the pretty heart of her femininity, he used his tongue in the way he knew she loved, enraptured with the melodious mews that escaped her throat and the scraping of her nails on his skull. He savoured her special, inimitable taste, the downiness of her hair, the silky texture of her skin, all unique to Chloe. Blindfold him and he would know her from the imprint of her mouth and the scent of her skin alone.

The nails scraping into his skull pulled at his hair, urging him on, her moans deepening, her breaths shallowing until she was crying out, his name spilling from her tongue and echoing through to his marrow.

Chloe sighed happily and gazed up at the stars while the stars Luis had set off in her twinkled with equal joy.

His touch alone was enough to soothe her. When he made love to her nothing else existed but them and the moment they were sharing.

So many moments. So many memories to take with her when they were over...

A pain sliced through her chest so sharp she gasped.

Luis, his wonderful mouth making its way back up her belly, must have assumed it was a gasp of pleasure for he took her breast into his mouth and encircled her nipple with his tongue in the way they had discovered she liked so much.

Fresh sensation building back up in her, Chloe closed her eyes and welcomed the pleasure, let it drown out the fleeting pain. When he reached her lips she kissed him greedily and looped her arms around him, needing to feel the solid warmth of his skin beneath her fingers.

She could have had the ton of lovers she'd once lied about but nothing would have compared to what she and Luis had. She didn't need to be experienced to know what they had was special and unique and belonged only to them.

She could drink his kisses for ever.

And, when he was finally inside her, fully sheathed, filling her completely, she wound her legs tightly around his waist and let go of everything but this most beautiful of moments.

CHAPTER ELEVEN

TINY SHARP PRICKLES dug into Chloe's cheek, as she roused into consciousness.

Absently running a hand over her face, she found sparkling grains of sand clinging to the pads of her fingers.

She smiled sleepily and rolled over, memories of Luis making love to her under the twinkling stars on the beach awakening other parts of her...

Luis shuffled in his sleep and groped for her hand.

She laced her fingers through his and stared at him. The sun had almost fully risen, its light filtering through the curtains. Luis's features were clear and strong. Thick dark stubble had broken through his skin since he'd shaved the morning before. When he had made love to her that stubble had scratched her breasts in a way that had been half pain and half pleasure.

Everything about them was like that. Half pain. Half pleasure.

So much had been revealed between them in the days they had spent on this island.

She felt wretched about the hand she had played in Benjamin's revenge.

It had been her revenge too, she had to acknowledge painfully.

Luis had never set out to cheat her brother.

He had kidnapped her and blackmailed her but that all felt like a lifetime ago, actions done to and conducted by two different people.

The man she had once believed herself in love with *did* exist.

And if he did exist then didn't that mean…?

That their marriage could be for real…?

'You've got that look on your face that tells me you are thinking,' he whispered, his voice thick with sleep.

She blinked, reopening her eyes to find his gorgeous hazel gaze fixed on her.

You don't want to know what I'm thinking.

Or maybe he did.

Maybe it wasn't just the desire they shared.

Oh, what was she *thinking*?

She would still be entering a marriage based on revenge.

But that had been agreed before they'd made love and before they'd opened up to each other.

Before she'd accepted that she loved him.

And even if his feelings for her were as strong as hers were for him, that didn't mean they had the basis of anything that could last.

Luis was a twin. He and his brother had a bond she could not begin to understand and it pained her to know that even if she and Luis were to have a proper future together, she would always come second to Javier.

This was a dream she didn't dare hope for.

'I'm just thinking it's been a few hours since you made love to me,' she whispered back, putting her hand on his cheek.

Her brain hurt from sleep deprivation and too much conversation. Now she was hallucinating thoughts.

Love?

No, that was taking things too far.

She felt a lot towards this man, but love…?

Proper, uninterrupted sleep was needed. Then,

when her brain and body were refreshed, she would be able to think properly.

But first she wanted the closeness she felt when he was deep inside her.

Snuggling into him, she welcomed his arms wrapping around her, a blanket in their own right, and closed her eyes to the heady power of his intoxicating kiss.

Sleep. Everything would look different after she'd had some.

Everything was the same.

Everything.

Chloe was lying on her back in the calm sea, Luis's arm acting as a float.

After making love and then falling into a deep, pure sleep, she had woken with the urge to swim. He hadn't questioned it—she didn't allow herself to think too deeply about it either—just led her to the section of beach where the water was calm and so clear she could see the tiny pebbles on its bed.

The most important part, he'd reiterated seriously, was being able to float. And to be able to float, she needed to relax in the water.

They had taken it slowly.

'Are you ready for me to remove my arm?' he asked.

The patience he'd shown in getting her to this stage filled her heart with the buoyancy she needed to stay afloat.

She trusted him. To not let her drown. To keep her alive.

With her heart.

For the better or the worse she did not know but loving Luis had changed something fundamental in her.

When he looked in her eyes she almost dared hope she saw the same reflected as shone from hers.

And if it wasn't there yet then she had to take the chance that one day it would be.

She had allowed her father to destroy her fragile heart for too long.

She had carried his rejection every day for seven years… No, she'd carried his rejection her entire life.

He was the reason she had kept men at arm's length, she'd come to realise. Her father had rejected her twice, the first time while she had still been in the womb. The second rejection had been the one that had destroyed her and shattered any trust she might have. She'd always told herself it was men she didn't trust but the truth, as she could now see clearly, was that her father's rejection of the almost fully grown-up Chloe had left her feeling inherently unlovable. If her own father couldn't find anything to love about her then why would anyone else?

Tomorrow she would exchange her vows with Luis. If she didn't take the chance and trust the passion and friendship that had grown between them then she would never find it with anyone else and she would grow into a lonely old woman.

There would never be anyone else for her.

She looked into Luis's eyes and smiled.

His eyes sparkled. 'Is that a yes?'

Her smile widened.

She couldn't speak. Not with words.

She loved him.

He let go.

She floated.

When Luis opened his eyes into the duskiness of early morning he thought for sure he was still sleeping. This had to be a dream. A wonderful, heady, sensuous dream.

Dreams of Chloe were nothing new. He'd woken with erotic dreams of them simmering in his blood so many times over the past few months that it was more a surprise when he didn't have them. The intensity of them had only grown since they had become lovers.

They never felt this real though.

He closed his eyes and hooked an arm above his head with a sigh.

Dios, that felt good.

Chloe was underneath the sheets, between his legs, pleasuring him with her tongue.

He groaned as she slid him into her mouth, groaning even louder when she cupped his...

Dios.

This was incredible.

In his dreams he was always left unfulfilled but now he could feel telltale sensations tugging at his loins.

And then she stopped.

This time his groan was one of frustration that was cut off from his tongue when she pulled the sheets off him and crawled over him.

Putting her hands either side of his face, she stared down at him with a soft gleam in her eyes. 'Good morning.'

And then she sank down on his burning erection.

Luis gasped.

There had been a very real danger then that he would have come undone with one thrust.

But, *Dios*, this was like nothing he had ever felt before. This was something new.

They had never made love without a condom before.

He had never made love without a condom before.

He could not have comprehended how different it would feel being completely bare inside her or the sensations that would course through his blood and loins.

Adjusting herself so she was sitting upright with him fully inside her, she rested her hands lightly on his chest.

Luis gazed at her, now quite certain that he wasn't dreaming and that this was real, that this was Chloe waking him in such a pleasurable way, Chloe, the woman he would be marrying that day.

He raised a hand to cover one of her breasts. *Dios*, he loved her breasts. Loved her soft, rounded belly. Loved her supple thighs currently squeezing against him. Loved the raven hair falling in waves over her breasts and down her back.

And then he loved when she began to take her pleasure from him, finding a rhythm, leaning forward to stare deep into his eyes as her breasts gently swayed with the motion.

He couldn't take his eyes from her face. Her eyes had darkened in colour, becoming violet, her cheeks slashed with the colour of passion. Harder and deeper she ground against him, tiny moans flying out of those gorgeous lips that became louder when he grabbed hold of her hips to steady her and drive himself up into her.

Colour heightened on her cheeks and then he felt her orgasm build inside her as vividly as he felt his own, her muscles thickening and tightening around him as, with a loud cry, she fell against him at the exact moment he lost all control of himself.

For long moments the world went white.

* * *

'We didn't use a condom,' he said a short while later when they had finally caught their breath.

He didn't know if it was an oversight on her part or if she had meant it.

He didn't know which he hoped the answer would be.

Since they had become lovers they had only ever used condoms, which he'd armed himself with from the numerous boxes he had thrown into his suitcase on a whim before he had kidnapped her. He made sure to always have some handy wherever he went, their passion for each other often finding them making love in the most unlikely places, like on the beach in the middle of the night.

Neither of them had mentioned her being on the pill since he had confronted her with the packet.

She was still on top of him.

He was still inside her.

She nuzzled into his neck. 'I know.'

Then she raised her head and put her chin to his.

The look in her eyes was one he had never seen before. 'I trust you, Luis.'

He forced a smile to lips that had become leaden.

The euphoria of the moment died as a klaxon set off in his guts at this declaration of trust that instinct told him meant much more than had been said.

In truth, he had felt that klaxon warming up since he had taken her swimming the day before.

There had been a moment when he had been encouraging her to try and float when she had looked in his eyes and he'd felt as if she had seen right down to his soul.

The only thing that made him certain she hadn't seen right down into it was that she hadn't run away screaming.

His yacht was on its way to the island, the captain and crew preparing for the ceremony that would make him and Chloe husband and wife. The press release had been prepared, the champagne was on ice, everything that could be controlled taken care of.

And yet he felt his control over the situation slipping through his fingers and he didn't know how to claw it back.

* * *

Luis pounded along the beach, stretching his legs as he jogged, running as he hadn't run in too many years to count.

He hadn't wanted to swim. He'd needed to do something physical that didn't remind him of the woman he'd left burrowed under the covers, her lips curved in a beautiful smile as she slept.

The sun rising over the Caribbean like an enormous jewel was a glorious sight but not one he could appreciate. The knots in his stomach were too tight for him to appreciate anything at that moment.

In a few hours he would be a married man to the most beautiful woman in the world.

Their marriage was supposed to be an exercise in damage limitation.

It was not supposed to feel like this.

He was not supposed to let her get close to him.

A short, entertaining marriage that fixed all the problems she had helped create. That was all it was supposed to be.

He was not supposed to feel her presence like a pulse.

How the hell she did it he did not know but

Chloe had a talent for drawing things out of himself that he'd hardly acknowledged to himself. She was better than any priest for making a man want to bear his rotten soul. Not even Benjamin knew he'd been his father's whipping boy.

He had never had to physically drag himself away from a woman before.

After running for an hour he headed back and went straight in the shower without checking in on her.

The knots in his stomach hadn't gone.

Almost ten miles of pounding his legs and he felt as out of sorts as when he'd set off.

Only when he had dried and dressed did he check his phone and find a missed call from his brother.

As if he didn't feel crap enough as it was.

Javier had ignored his calls since that disastrous video conference with the Canadian. He'd messaged him a few times about the business but voice-to-voice conversations had been blacklisted.

His brother really could be a cold bastard when he wanted. Add injured pride—and Javier's pride had been enormously injured by Benjamin steal-

ing his fiancée away from him and in such a deliberate and public manner—and his brother was
a tinderbox primed to explode.

Luis wanted to help him but had learned
through their thirty-five years together that there
was no point in putting pressure on his twin to
see reason. When he was in a mood like this it
was best to keep his distance and wait either for
Javier to open up or for the darkness to pass.

With a heavy sigh, he stepped out onto the bal-
cony and called Javier back.

'Why are you with Chloe Guillem?' Javier
asked, not even bothering with a cursory greet-
ing.

'I am saving our backsides,' Luis informed him
calmly. He had hoped to have this conversation
after the deed was done. He'd known from the
outset that his brother would not approve this
plan of action. How he had discovered that he
was with Chloe was a mystery to be solved another time.

'By getting involved with that poisonous bitch?'

'Do not speak of her in that way,' Luis cut in,
his hackles rising at the insult to Chloe.

She was the least poisonous woman he knew.

'She is a Guillem. Everything they touch is poison.'

Luis counted to ten before responding.

He had to remember that it was Javier's fiancée Benjamin had stolen away with Chloe's assistance. For Javier, it ran much more deeply.

'I'm marrying her today. Having Chloe as my wife will prove to the world that the rumours of what happened between us and Benjamin are unfounded. George will be placated. It will save the Canadian project and kill the rumours flying around about us.'

'I don't care about any of that.'

'We have already invested fifty million euros in it. That's money we will never get back. Investors on other projects are asking questions too. I'm not telling you anything you don't already know.'

'The other investors won't do anything, you'll see. It will blow over and, even if it doesn't, I would rather take the financial hit than have a Guillem marry into our family.'

'Don't be so petty. I'm saving our business by doing this.' He almost added that marrying Chloe was an excellent form of revenge on Benjamin but stopped himself at the last moment.

It felt like a lifetime ago that revenge had been the driving force behind all this.

When had that motive disappeared?

He shrugged the thought away and concentrated on the conversation at hand.

'Our backsides don't need saving any more than our business does. Our fortune is safe. We might take a short-term hit but we can claw the long-term back, and we can preserve our reputations by other means.'

'*What* other means?' Luis demanded to know.

'We would have thought of something already if you hadn't gone running off on this hare-brained scheme.'

'You were not in the mood to talk,' Luis reminded him with equal venom. 'Need I remind you that your whole attitude was to sit and seethe with only yourself for company?'

'I was thinking.'

'And I was doing. Marrying Chloe is the best solution for everyone.'

'Have you lost your mind?' his brother demanded with incredulity. 'We have overcome worse than this by working together and putting on a united front. That's all we need to do. Ride it out. We don't need her and I cannot believe you would think otherwise. That woman conspired with her brother to destroy us and now you want to marry her into our family? No, you *have* lost your mind, and over a *woman*...' His disgust was clear to hear. 'Has her pretty face blinded you to her poison?'

'Do not be ridiculous,' Luis snarled, the end of his tether reached. 'Chloe regrets the part she played and wants to put things right.'

'You *defend* her?' Javier's laughter was hollow. 'Marry her if you must but do not pretend it's for our sake. We do not need her to get through this and for you to think otherwise only proves your head has been turned.'

Then the line went dead.

Anger fisting in his guts, Luis threw his phone on the floor.

How dared his own twin question his judgement in such a way? And as for saying he'd lost his mind over Chloe...

Luis accepted that he'd let her get closer than he'd ever intended but he had not lost his head. He could walk away from her right now and not feel an ounce of regret.

In an instant the anger was replaced by a wave of relief so strong he could almost see the ripples in the air as it left his shoulders, all the tension and knots that had grown in him these past few days leaving with it.

Javier was wrong about his feelings for Chloe but in one respect he *was* right.

It always had been the two of them, the Casillas brothers against the world. Everything the cruel world had thrown at them had been faced and defeated together. Why should this situation be any different?

And why had it taken so long for him to recognise it?

Whatever the reason, his relief was absolute.

He didn't have to marry Chloe.

CHAPTER TWELVE

CHLOE STEPPED OUT of the bathroom with only a towel around her. Luis was sitting on the edge of the bed.

One look at his face told her something was wrong.

'What's the matter?' She walked to her dressing table to put her watch on.

'Nothing's wrong. Quite the opposite.'

'What are you talking about?'

'Our wedding is off.'

She laughed. 'Funny. You should be a comedian.'

'Our wedding is off. I've let the captain know. I've had a helicopter flown in which will transport us to Lisa Island and...'

'Are you being *serious*?' she interrupted.

'Yes.'

She searched his face. 'But why? Is it something I've done?'

'No, *bonita*. You have done nothing wrong. *Au contraire*, as you would say. I have spoken to Javier. We are in agreement that it is unnecessary for me to marry you. We have decided to proceed as we have always done; together, putting on a united front to the world. Be happy. You can be out of my life sooner than you had hoped.'

Chloe felt the blood drain from her face. It happened so quickly she had to grab hold of the dressing table tightly as the room began to spin.

It took a few goes before she could open her throat enough to speak and when she did, her words were croaky. 'Our marriage is no longer necessary?'

'I apologise for wasting your time.'

'Are you for real? Is this a joke?' This absolutely did not make sense. The look on his face did not make sense, a mixture of lightness and grimness, a strange combination that terrified her.

'I am for real and this is not a joke.' He got to his feet. 'The helicopter will leave here in an hour and I've arranged for a jet to take you from Lisa Island back to Grand Bahama. Let me know when you wish to fly back to Europe and I will get that arranged for you too.'

He headed out of the bedroom door, hands in pockets, as nonchalant as if he'd just told her breakfast was about to be served.

This could not be happening.

This *was* happening.

Violent storms churned in her belly, hot and cold darts bouncing in her dazed head.

Forcing her newly leaden legs to move and holding tightly to her towel, Chloe hurried out of the room behind him. 'Wait just one minute.'

He couldn't end it like this. No. This was all wrong. Not now, not after everything.

He was halfway down the corridor.

'Wait just one minute,' she repeated, raising her voice so he could not pretend to ignore her.

He stopped.

'Why are you doing this?'

'I just explained it to you.'

'No, you didn't. And please show me the courtesy of looking at me when you are speaking to me.'

He didn't move. 'I thought you would be happy.'

'Will you turn around and *look* at me?' she begged. 'Please, Luis, just look at me. *Talk* to me.'

If she had something to hand to throw at him to compel him to turn and face her she would take it gladly.

She needed to look in his eyes, really look, make sense of this grenade he had just thrown at her feet.

All she had was her towel.

He slowly turned.

When she finally got to look in his eyes she quailed.

There was nothing to read in them.

The shutters had come down and locked themselves shut.

'You only agreed to marriage because I blackmailed you,' he reminded her steadily, his frame like a statue. 'Neither of us wanted it.'

'I don't care about the marriage. I care that you're walking away from *us* without a word of discussion about it.'

'*Bonita*, there is no us. There never was.'

'Then what was the last week all about? That felt like an *us* to me.'

She had seen tenderness in his eyes. She had felt his tenderness in his kisses.

Surely, surely that hadn't all been a lie? Surely she hadn't dreamt it all up?

Her brain clouded in a steamy fog as she realised what she had done.

She had allowed herself to dream.

A fiery burn stabbed the back of her retinas and she blinked rapidly, driving the tears back, begging them not to fall, not to humiliate her.

'I am not responsible for your feelings,' he told her in that same steady voice. 'We were both very clear that our marriage would be a temporary arrangement to quell the stories and preserve my business. Javier and I...'

'Was it *him*?' Ice plunged into her spine at the mention of that hateful man, the ripples driving out the fog in her brain and bringing her to a form of clarity.

She believed Luis had had nothing to do with her brother signing the contract under false pretences but she would bet her brother's chateau that Javier had known.

'Talking to Javier made me see that this route was unnecessary. I acted rashly in demanding marriage from you. I should have thought things through in more detail but I was angry. Your brother had declared war on us.' He shrugged, a nonchalant, dismissive gesture that had her clenching her hands into fists. 'As regretful as it is with hindsight, anger leads to impulsive actions.'

She stared at him, trying her hardest to get air into her lungs. 'So I've given you all of this for nothing?'

'All of what?'

The tears she had come so close to shedding were sucked away as fury finally cut its way through the anguish.

She dropped her towel and held her arms out. 'This! Me!'

Let him see her naked. Let him see what he had taken, what she had given him, the very thing she had never given to anyone. Let him see her heart beating so frenziedly beneath her skin and the chest struggling to get air into it.

Let him see *her*.

Finally there was a flicker of something in his eyes.

'Oh, you liked this part, didn't you?' She laughed

mirthlessly. 'You couldn't get enough of it. I bet you were laughing through your teeth every time you made love to me. But there was no love in it, was there? It was all just *sex* to you—'

'Chloe,' he tried to cut in, but she was on a roll, anger and humiliation and a splintering heart too much to bear with any form of stoicism.

'Was it all a joke the pair of you dreamt up? Did I give you my virginity as part of a screwed-up *game*?'

His face contorted. 'You are making too much of this. We were never going to be for ever.'

'Of course we weren't going to be for ever. You don't do for ever, do you? Too busy hiding your feelings, scared someone will see too deeply and think the same as your father did. That's what scares you, isn't it?'

'How dare you?' The statue suddenly came to life with a roar.

'No, how dare *you*? How dare you make love to me like I mean something, how dare you comfort me, how dare you confide in me, how dare you make me dream when dreams were something I had given up?' Aware of angry tears splashing down her cheeks, she swiped them away.

'I have never lied to you,' he snarled, storming over to stand before her, as tall and as broad as she had ever seen him. 'You are the one who has made too much of what we've shared here. How would you have liked me to make love to you? With indifference?'

'I wish I'd never let you touch me in the first place!'

'But you did, didn't you?' He took hold of her chin roughly but painlessly and stared at her with eyes that spat fury. 'Do not blame me for *your* desires. We were never going to last. We've had fun together—I admit, I never expected to enjoy our time here as much as I have but now it is over. All I'm doing is bringing the end date forward and allowing us to pick up our lives.'

Chloe's open hand was inches from connecting with his hateful face before she became aware that she was on the verge of slapping him.

Even with all the hurt and fury unravelling like a nightmare kaleidoscope inside her she could not bring herself to physically harm him, not now, not with the tales of his father's violence so fresh in her mind.

What kind of a person would that make her?

She had lashed out at Luis before and he'd over-powered her easily but that meant nothing.

If she struck her hand to him that would make her as bad as the dead man she hated.

She *wanted* to hurt him. But not like that.

She would rather rip her own heart out than strike him in anger again.

Taking a deep breath, she dropped her hand and, with all the dignity she could muster in her naked state, looked him straight in the eye.

'You call what we have shared *fun*? Fun is for the parties you like to throw and for the women whose beds you hop in and out of without a care. I bared my soul to you. I confided things in you that I have never shared with anyone because I trusted you. I deserve better than to be discarded like an unwanted puppy that's outgrown its cute-ness.'

But the dignity was fleeting for as soon as she had said her piece she could feel the bones in her legs begin to crumble.

Terrified he would see the depths of her pain, Chloe turned on her heel and fled back to the bedroom.

The door shut with a bang loud enough to damage the hinges.

Luis closed his eyes and blew out a long puff of air.

After taking a few moments to gather his composure and rub his forehead to lessen the forming headache, he bent down to pick up Chloe's discarded towel. Discarded as she claimed he was discarding her.

He'd known she would be shocked that he was ending things so abruptly but never had he expected her to react like that.

He hadn't expected to see the pain in those blue eyes.

Dios, his head was really hurting.

Slinging her towel over his shoulder, he headed down the stairs to the kitchen and poured himself a glass of water and scavenged for painkillers. He found a packet stuck in the back of one drawer and popped the tablets out.

This was not his fault, he thought angrily. He was guilty of many things—kidnap, blackmail; the pain in his chest deepened just to think of it—but he had never led her on. Not by word or deed had he done anything to indicate he wanted a future with her.

She should be grateful. Better he ended it now, before she looked hard enough at him and she saw the rottenness that lay in his core. She'd alluded to it, to his father, but how she couldn't see it already was beyond him. He had kidnapped her. He had blackmailed her.

And she acted as if he'd wounded her by setting her free early.

He tossed the pills down his throat and drank the water. Maybe they would help the pain that had erupted in his chest as well as his head.

He should never have let it get this far. He should have worked harder to keep things on a purely physical level as he had always done before. Maybe then the sting of her words wouldn't feel so acute.

Hearing footsteps on the stairs, he braced himself for another onslaught.

Chloe appeared in the doorway.

She'd thrown on the shorts and red T-shirt she'd been wearing the day he had kidnapped her and had her beach bag stuffed tightly under her arm.

She walked to him, her gait stiff, stopping far

enough away that there was no danger in either of them touching, accidentally or not.

'I apologise for bringing your father into it,' she said tightly. 'That was uncalled for.'

He inhaled deeply then inclined his head. His throat had closed.

But what could he say? There was nothing left *to* say. Everything that could be said had already been said.

'I would be grateful if you would allow me to travel on my own in the helicopter,' she said into the silence, no longer looking at him.

By the time his throat had opened enough for him to speak, Chloe had walked out of the front door.

He let her go.

Chloe opened the letter with a shaking hand.

The large padded envelope had the official Compania de Ballet de Casillas logo embossed on it. It had been forwarded from her shared apartment in Madrid to the house she was currently staying at in London, where she had taken sanctuary with her old friend, Tanya. She hadn't called it sanctuary, of course, had said only that she was taking a break and begged use of Tanya's spare room.

Inside the envelope was a letter of reference written by Maria, the Head of Costume.

It was a glowing reference too.

She held it to her chest and blinked back tears.

Luis had authorised this for her. He must have done. Maria, as wonderful as she was, would not dare write a reference for her without permission.

Chloe hadn't asked for a reference. She'd assumed that there was no chance of her getting one, not after she had quit without working her notice and then for her hand in stealing their principal dancer away from the co-owner. She'd assumed her name would be mud in the whole company.

A separate, smaller envelope had fallen out of the package and landed by her feet. She picked it up, opened it and pulled out a goodbye card signed by the entire costume department and many of the other backstage crew. Even a few of the dancers had scribbled their names in it. There was also a personal handwritten note from Maria wishing her all the best for the future and telling her to seek her out the next time she was in Madrid.

The postscript at the end was what got her heart truly racing.

My daughter was going to have this ticket but she can no longer attend. It's yours. Please come.

Tucked in the envelope was a ticket for the opening night of Compania de Ballet de Casillas's new theatre.

Chloe resisted the instinct to rip it in two.

Instead, she placed it on her dressing table and pinched the bridge of her nose to keep the tears at bay.

She'd cried too much in the past month.

The worst of it was that she couldn't tell anyone, not even Tanya.

How could she admit that she'd been stupid enough to fall in love with the man who'd kidnapped her and blackmailed her? They would think she was suffering a version of Stockholm syndrome.

She wished she could explain her pain away on that. That would be easier to cope with.

Easier to cope with than to accept that she, the woman who had learned the hard way that dreams did not come true, had allowed herself to dream of a future with a man incapable of returning her love.

The flash of cameras that went off as Luis stepped out of the limousine with his brother would have blinded a less practised man.

Unfazed, the Casillas brothers cut their way through the reporters all eager for a sound bite, past the chanting crowd all hoping to spot a famous face, and up the stairs and through the theatre's doors.

The new theatre that homed Compania de Ballet de Casillas was, Luis thought with satisfaction, a perfect blend of new and old. They had employed the best architect to work on it, Daniele Pellegrini, and he had produced the same magic that had won him so many awards through the years.

The fifteen-hundred-strong audience crowded inside were enjoying a drink in one of the five bars or finding their seats, excited chatter filling the magnificent bowled space. He and Javier had made the conscious decision to give only a third of the tickets to VIPs. The remaining two thirds had been sold through a form of lottery, reasonably priced so any member of the public should be able to afford it, something they both felt strongly about, that the arts should not be the domain of the rich. Every member of the audience, whether rich or poor, had made an effort with their appearance and it warmed his cold heart to see the glittering dresses, smart suits and tuxedos.

The press were out in force, not from a desire to see the theatre's grand opening or to review the performance of *The Red Shoes*—although the bona fide critics had been allocated seats— but because two of the parties of the love triangle would be under the same roof for the first time since Benjamin had stolen Freya two months ago.

It would be the first time Javier had come face to face with the woman who had dumped him so publicly.

The tension emanating from his brother's huge shoulders let Luis know the strain Javier was under. He hadn't loved Freya but his pride had suffered an enormous blow.

It would not be easy for Javier to see the woman he'd intended to marry dancing on his stage, the star of the performance. Despite the animosity that curdled between them, Luis felt for him.

Things had been strained between the brothers since Luis had returned from the Caribbean. They continued to work together, conducted their regular meetings, nothing changed in that respect, but a coldness had developed between them, unlike anything they had been through before.

However, Javier had been correct that they would get through the bad press that had been unleashed on them. They'd written the Canadian project off—damn, that had felt great telling that sanctimonious oaf George where to go—and it had generated the expected flurry of headlines. But with all the parties in the Javier, Benjamin and Freya love triangle remaining tight-lipped, the press had run out of new angles for the story. The ever-moving news cycle had moved on to new fodder…until that evening.

Although this was an opinion he chose not to share with his brother, Luis was grateful that Freya had some loyalty left in her. She had, naturally, handed her notice in with Compania de Ballet de Casillas but had agreed to honour her commitment to this opening performance. They kept their star performer for one last night and, without actually saying a word, Freya was telling the world that they couldn't be the complete monsters the cruel Internet commentators gleefully insisted they must be.

Whenever Luis thought of those comments now, he thought of Chloe. She had been far more outraged by them than he had been. It was as if she had taken them personally.

Sometimes, alone in his bed, Luis would gaze at the ceiling and wonder where the madness had come from that had made him think marrying her would be the solution to all their problems.

His brother had been right: he *had* lost his mind.

And then he would stop thinking.

Or try to stop thinking.

He couldn't rid himself of her. Everywhere he went his mind played tricks on him. He'd walked past the coffee shop where he had first been so dazzled by her and had seen her in there, laughing, her raven hair flowing like waves around her. And then he'd blinked and she'd gone.

Drinks in hand, faking cordiality, he and Javier settled themselves in their private box, which they had chosen to share that evening with senior members of the Spanish royal family. Sitting on his other side was a ravishing princess. Four months ago he would have decided on the spot to get her into bed. Now he couldn't even muster basic interest.

There had been no one since he had left the Caribbean. Not even a twitch in his loins. There had been no one other than Chloe since their one date all those months ago…

The curtains fell back and the performance began.

Within minutes Luis experienced his usual boredom when watching the ballet. He much preferred watching an action-packed movie to this, and he found his gaze drifting over the audience.

Minutes before the interval, he saw, hidden at the back of the box on the other side of the theatre, the unmistakable dark features of Benjamin Guillem.

Putting his binoculars to his eyes, he trained them on him to confirm it.

Yes, it was Benjamin.

Luis had not expected him to be there. Indeed, if he were a gambling man he would have put his money on Benjamin staying away.

Admiration flickered in him. Benjamin had voluntarily entered the lion's den. That took balls...

And then he saw the expression on his old friend's face and moved the binoculars to the stage where Freya was dancing a solo. Then he trained them back on Benjamin and he understood, his heart suddenly thumping rapidly, why he had come.

He was there to support the woman he loved.

Luis's thoughts flashed to Chloe.

His thoughts *always* flashed to Chloe.

'What is she doing here?' Javier hissed in his ear. He too was looking through his binoculars.

'Who?' He would not mention Benjamin's presence.

'Chloe.'

Whipping his binoculars to where his brother's

were trained, high up in the gods, Luis sucked in a breath as he worked on the lens's focus.

He made sure to blink before looking again, certain that his eyes were playing their familiar trick on him.

Dios, it was her, ravishing in a black lace dress, her raven hair framing her face in a sleek, coiffured style he had never seen before but which enhanced her elfin beauty.

'What is she doing here?' Javier repeated.

'I don't know.'

He had no idea where she had got a ticket from or why she had come.

Or why his heart hammered so hard his ribs vibrated with the force.

CHAPTER THIRTEEN

CHLOE WATCHED THE performance without paying any attention to what was happening on the stage. She managed to keep her frame still but emotionally she was all over the place.

She had a good view of the Casillas brothers' private box and had spotted Luis the moment he'd entered it. That one look had been enough for her heart to set off at a thrum and for her palms to become clammy.

That one look had been enough to prove she had made an enormous mistake in coming here.

On one side of him sat his hateful brother. On the other side a beautiful woman dressed in crushed velvet whispering intimately into his ear.

Chloe had put her binoculars back in her clutch bag and refused to look in his direction again.

What was she trying to prove to herself? she thought miserably as the performance went on. That she was over him?

The ticket had been sitting on her dressing table for a week when, after another terrible night's sleep, she had decided to go.

She needed to see him one last time, in circumstances over which *she* was in control.

She'd had it all planned out. She would find him during the interval or the after-show party—she knew enough people to be confident of someone helping her sneak in—and then she would graciously thank him for the reference and sweep out with all the grace she had been practising all week.

It destroyed her to know his last memory of her was as an hysterical wreck.

She hadn't even cared that coming here would mean she would see Javier or that there was the chance she would bump into her brother. She hadn't seen Benjamin since she'd returned to Europe.

Her wounds were too fresh for her to see anyone who cared enough to notice the insomnia-inflicted bruising beneath her eyes. Tanya cared but she was busy with her work and still the party animal of old. In Tanya's home, Chloe found the peace she craved but also the time she'd always shied away from that allowed her to think.

Oh, what had she come here for?

More humiliation?

Luis didn't love her. He wouldn't care that she had made a deliberate effort with her appearance or for any graceful sweep away from him. She would have been relegated to his past. She doubted he'd given her more than a fleeting thought, other than arranging her reference.

She had to do what he had always said and look to the future. She could do nothing about the past but she could pick her life up and move forward. She could complete the application form for the ballet company in New York and make a fresh start.

Another fresh start.

But this would be the last.

She wouldn't go chasing a dream; she would create her own.

Suddenly filled with determination, she straightened her spine and waited for the performance to end.

How Luis remained in his seat through the rest of the performance he would never know. He kept his binoculars trained on Chloe, willing her to look his way.

But she didn't. Her eyes stayed fixed on the drama unfolding on the stage, oblivious to his presence and oblivious to the drama unfolding in the pit of his stomach.

Dios, she looked so beautiful. The way she was holding herself too… When they'd been together she had been a great one for slouching and putting her feet up wherever she went. Tonight she looked as regal as the princess sitting beside him, who had given up her attempts to draw him into conversation.

It must have taken real guts for Chloe to come here tonight.

Which begged the question of why she had come. Was it merely that she'd procured an invitation and, being a ballet lover, had decided to use it? That was the only logical explanation he could think of. He hadn't seen or spoken to her in over a month.

Whatever her reasons, the Guillems had more guts than an ice-hockey team. Both of them had entered the lion's den.

But Benjamin had entered it to support the woman he loved.

After the way things had ended between him and Chloe he could say with one hundred per cent confidence that she was not there to support him.

But she was there.

And he couldn't take his eyes off her.

And he couldn't fight the knots in his stomach that were pulling tighter and tighter in him.

'I'm going to have a word with Security and make sure they know not to let her into the after-party,' Javier murmured as they rose to their feet at the end of the performance.

As Luis was craning his neck to keep watch over Chloe, it took a few moments to understand what his brother was saying.

He turned his attention to him. 'You will leave her alone,' he said sharply.

Javier's face darkened into something ugly. 'You still defend her? After what she did?'

'She was defending her brother, doing what either you or I would do if we felt someone had hurt us.'

Their royal guests had got to their feet.

Remembering his manners, Luis managed to exchange a few words with them as they exited the box.

Right at the last moment he turned his head for one last sight of Chloe but found her row empty.

Swallowing back the bile that had risen up his throat, he forced a smile to his lips and joined the throng in the corridor.

The after-show party was being held in one of the theatre's underground conference rooms and, trying hard to keep his attention on his honoured guests and not allow his eyes to keep darting about in the hope of catching a glimpse of a raven-haired beauty, Luis headed to it.

When the group took a left where the corridor forked, he saw, in the distance, the tall figure of Benjamin.

Not hesitating for a moment, Luis put his hand on his brother's back and steered him in the other direction, calling over his shoulder to their guests that they would join them shortly.

'What's the matter?' Javier asked, staring at him with suspicion as they walked.

'I wanted to talk to you alone.'

He hadn't realised until he said the words that he *did* want to speak to his brother.

Avoiding a confrontation with Benjamin was the impetus he needed to confront his brother with a conversation they should have had a long time ago.

'You knew we were ripping Benjamin off all those years ago, didn't you?'

It was the first time Luis had vocalised this notion.

His brother's face darkened. 'We didn't rip him off. He was the fool who signed the contract without reading it.'

'And you should have warned him the terms had changed as you'd said you would do. You didn't forget, did you?'

His brother merely glowered in response.

'I knew it.' Luis took a deep breath, trying hard to contain the nausea swirling inside him that was fighting with a swell of rage. 'All these years and I've told myself that it had been an oversight on your part when I should have accepted the truth that you never forget. In thirty-five years you have never forgotten anything or failed to do something you promised.'

'I never promised to email him.'

'Not an actual promise,' Luis conceded. 'But look me in the eye and tell me it wasn't a deliberate act on your part.'

But all he saw in his twin's eyes was a black hardness.

'For what reason would it have been deliberate?' Javier asked with a sneer.

'That is for your conscience to decide. All I know for sure is that Benjamin was our friend. I have defended you and I have fought your corner...'

'*Our* corner,' Javier corrected icily. 'I assume this burst of conscience from you is connected to that damned woman.'

His temper finally getting the better of him, Luis grabbed his brother by the collar of his shirt. 'If you ever speak about Chloe in that way again then you and I are finished. Do you hear me? Finished.'

'If you're still defending her to me then I would say we're already finished, *brother.*' He spat the last word directly into Luis's face.

Eyeball to eyeball, they glowered at each other,

the venom seeping between them thick enough to taste.

Then Luis released his hold, stepped back and unclenched the fist he hadn't been aware of making.

His eyes still fixed on the man he had shared a womb with, had shared a bedroom with, had fought with, had protected, had been protected by, had grieved with, the other side of the coin that was the Casillas twins, Luis took backwards strides until he could look no more and turned his back on his brother for the last time.

With long strides, Luis walked the theatre's corridors, hardening his heart to what he had just walked away from, his focus now on one thing only: finding Chloe.

He had the rest of his life to sort out his relationship with Javier. And if they couldn't sort it out? He would handle it.

An incessant nagging in his guts told him he had only one opportunity to make things right with the woman it had taken him far too long to realise he was in love with. He did not think he could handle it if his attempts didn't work.

As he picked up his pace, scanning the crowds ahead for a tall, raven-haired woman, he collided with a much smaller blonde woman with a face he vaguely recognised.

'Sorry,' he muttered.

'My fault,' she whispered, looking over his shoulder. 'I wasn't looking where I was going.'

Forgetting all about her, he continued to scour the corridors and bars, put his head into the conference room where the after-show party was being held three times, until he had a burst of inspiration and hurried to the costume department.

By the time he reached it, he was out of breath.

He pushed the door open and there she was, chatting with Maria over a bottle of wine.

Both women looked at him, startled at his appearance.

Only Chloe turned a deep red colour to match her lipstick to see him there.

'Maria, can I have a minute alone with Chloe, please?' he asked as politely as he could.

She must have read something on his face for she shot to her feet and hurried out of the door. 'I'll be at the party,' she murmured as she closed the door behind her.

'Can I have some of that?' he asked, nodding at the bottle of white wine.

Chloe handed him her glass without a word.

He drained it and handed it back to her. 'I was thirsty,' he said in an attempt at humour that failed when her lips didn't move.

And then they did move. 'I'm here legitimately. I was given a ticket.'

'I'm not here to question your legitimacy.' He took Maria's vacated seat and rolled his shoulders.

Chloe pushed her chair back, away from him. 'Then why are you here? I assume you've been looking for me.'

'I saw you from my seat.'

'I saw you too. You looked very cosy. Have you abandoned your date?'

'I don't have a date,' he said, confused.

She raised her brow and pursed her lips.

Then he understood who she meant and gave a hollow laugh. 'The women who sat with us are members of the royal family. We invited them to share our box out of courtesy. There is nothing in it.'

'I wouldn't care if there was.'

But he recognised the look he'd seen fleetingly on her face from the times he had mentioned Marietta, before she had realised Marietta was nearly ninety years old. It was the first time he recognised that look as jealousy.

That jealousy allowed him to breathe a little more easily.

'How have you been?' he asked.

'I've been having a great time in London, thank you.'

'London?'

'Yes. I've been there since I left the Caribbean and I'm flying back there in the morning. Now, did you seek me out to make small talk or was there a purpose to it?'

'Have mercy on me, *bonita*. I know I don't deserve it but allow me the small talk. What I have to say is hard for me. I need to build up to it.'

She looked at her watch.

Was he imagining it or did it look loose on her wrist?

Had she lost weight?

'My cab is collecting me in thirty minutes. I will need ten minutes to get to the front, which gives you twenty minutes to say what you need to say.'

'I can give you a lift to wherever you want to go.' Hopefully home with him.

Unmoved, she looked again at her watch and said pointedly, 'Twenty minutes.'

He nodded and took a deep breath. 'Okay. Did you get the reference?'

'Yes. Thank you for arranging that. I assume you authorised it?'

'I did. And now I would like you to rip it up and return to Madrid.'

'You want me to come back and work for you?'

'No, I want you to come back and be my wife.'

There was a moment of silence before a grin broke out on her face. It didn't meet her eyes and there was no humour in it. 'You really are a co-median.'

He cursed under his breath. 'I am not being funny, *bonita*. I want you to marry me.'

'And I am not being funny either, but if you call me *bonita* one more time I will pour the contents of the bottle over your head.' The fake smile dropping, she got to her feet. 'Excuse me but I don't have time for any more of your games.'

He managed to take hold of her hand before she could snatch it away.

'Please, sit down. I'm not playing games. I know I am doing this all wrong but I have never told someone I love them before.'

Her eyes widened, a pulse ringing through them before she blinked all expression out of them.

Snatching her hand from his, she said, 'I thought Javier was the cruel one.'

'He is cruel,' Luis agreed sombrely. 'Our childhoods screwed with our heads. He has to live with seeing our father's reflection every time he looks in the mirror.'

'And how did it screw with yours?'

'I have to live with seeing the reflection my father hated.'

She studied him in silence then carefully sat back down. 'I have to live with seeing the reflection my father didn't want every day,' she said slowly.

He couldn't tell if she was relaying this as a fact or to empathise. Her usually melodious tones were flatter than he had ever heard them.

'I know you do. How you have turned into such a vivacious and loving woman is inspiring. You could be bitter with the world but you're not. People like you.'

'People like you too,' she pointed out.

'They like my money. They like the parties I host and the presents I give. I've had to buy my friendships.'

Something flickered in her eyes. 'That's not true. You've always been a fun person to be around.'

'I like to have fun,' he conceded. 'But I am talking of real friendship. You and Benjamin are the only people other than my brother that I have been able to let my guard down with.'

'Because you have known us all your life?'

'With Benjamin, yes. We grew up together. He knew me before the nightmare, but you were just a child then and remained a child in my eyes until you came to Madrid and I suddenly saw the beautiful, vibrant woman you had become. I looked at you with brand-new eyes and I fell in love, and I never even knew it. I ended our date filled with emotions I can't explain because I have never felt them before, and then everything blew up with your brother and you, rightly, didn't want to know me any more. Through all the litigation we were going through, you were always there in my mind. I couldn't stop thinking about you. When you called me to say you had broken down in the mountains... *Dios*, I have never driven so fast in my life. To learn it had been a trick to get me away from the gala...ah, *bonita*, I was furious—please don't pour the wine over me—but my revenge was never focused where it should have been, on your brother, but on *you*.'

He paused for breath and gave a shake of his head. 'Javier says I lost my mind insisting that you married me and now I can see that he was right. Of course, back then I didn't see it—in truth, it's only becoming clear to me now as I say it to you.'

'Truth?' she said with only the slightest hint of cynicism. 'You're saying you kidnapped me and blackmailed me because you love me? Do you have any idea how screwed up that sounds?'

He ran a hand through his hair. 'Don't you know by now that I *am* a screw-up?'

'Then explain this. If you did all that because you love me, why did you end it so cruelly?'

'I was scared,' he replied simply. 'What I felt for you was like nothing I had ever felt for anyone. It scared the hell out of me. And I was scared that you were falling in love with me, scared that if you fell much harder you would see me too clearly.'

'I did see you clearly,' she said slowly. 'I always did. Even when I hated you I understood you. I understood you more when I learned about your relationship with your father. In many ways we are kindred spirits, two children longing for love from a parent who refused to give it. I fell in love with you when I was seventeen years old. I dreamed of marrying you…and then I grew up and learned the truth of my conception and had to come to terms with my father…' She took her own deep breath. 'But you know all this. I confided it in you. I had never told a soul. No one knew. It was too raw and too personal but I entrusted it with you.'

'You were in love with me all that time?' he asked in dazed disbelief.

'All that time.' Her smile was sad. 'You were there for all of us when we most needed you. You made my mother smile on the days she was so ill and so low from her treatment that she could hardly lift her head. You brought joy to all our lives and then on the day we buried her, when I so desperately needed someone to hold onto, you were there to hold me up and give me the strength to keep going. Of course I fell in love with you. Over the years I thought my love for you had…not died but been put aside with all my other childish things. And then I saw you again in Madrid and all my old feelings for you erupted.

'When Benjamin told me about the contract it broke my heart. I couldn't understand how you could be there for us during the worst time of our lives and at the same time conspire against us. Of course, I know differently now and as soon as I accepted that I had been wrong, my love for you… Luis, it never died. It's always been with me.'

He sighed. He couldn't hide it from her, not now that he knew the truth. 'Javier did know.'

'What do you mean?'

'When he didn't warn your brother about the change in the profit terms… It was a deliberate act. He didn't forget.'

'I know that.'

Unsure if he understood her correctly, he clarified, 'You know? How?'

She shrugged. 'Benjamin was adamant he mentioned the terms of profit on the night it was signed and that nothing was said to the contrary. That's why he felt so betrayed and why I felt so betrayed. If it wasn't said to you it must have been Javier.'

'I'm sorry.'

'You are not your brother. And he's paid for his deception. I'm sorry you were dragged into it.'

'Don't be. I kept my mouth shut for seven years and ignored the nagging voice that told me Javier's actions had been deliberate.'

'I can't say I wouldn't have done the same if I had been in your shoes. What you two have lived through together…' Her sigh was heavy as she got to her feet and looked at her watch. 'He's your brother. Your loyalty is to him. I understand that. I always have.'

As she headed to the door, he suddenly realised what she was doing and stood, kicking his chair back so forcefully it fell onto its side.

'Where are you going?'

'To my cab. I'm already running late for it.'

'You're *leaving*?'

She closed her eyes and nodded.

'But…' He groped for words, unable to comprehend this turn of events, not after the heartfelt exchange they'd just had that had alternately ripped his soul from him and cleansed it.

'I told you I would be getting a cab, Luis,' she said softly. 'I'm sorry. I can't marry you.'

She could not be serious. Please, God, do not let her be serious. 'You just told me that you love me.'

'I *do* love you but it's not enough. Don't you understand?'

'No,' he answered flatly, walking over to her, trying his hardest to quell the rising panic in his chest. Putting his hand on the nape of her neck, he brought his forehead to hers. 'I love you, you love me, what else is there to understand? You are my heart. Do you understand *that*? I have spent the past six weeks feeling as if something inside me has died and it was only when I saw you in the audience tonight that I realised what was wrong with me. *You* were what's wrong. I love you, more than anything or anyone.'

'I'm sorry,' she repeated, blinking frantically. She slipped out of his hold and wrapped her finger around the door handle. 'Please don't come any closer. I'm sorry. You hurt me too much. I've been in agony without you and have only just patched myself back together. I can't go through that again. I love you but I don't trust that you won't break my heart again. Forgive me.'

Ready to argue some more, to fight, to make every promise that would make her see sense, Luis caught the look in her eyes and closed his mouth.

What little fight was left in him vanished.

The pain he saw reflecting back at him was too acute to argue with.

He could gift-wrap his heart for her and she wouldn't believe it.

Their eyes stayed locked together, a thousand emotions passing between them before she gave a small nod of her head, raised her shoulders and walked out of the room.

Slumping against the door, Luis listened to the click-clack of her shoes fade away to nothing.

And then he fell to the floor and buried his face in his hands, every wretched part of him feeling as if it were being pulled through every circle of Dante's hell.

* * *

Chloe walked as fast as she dared on heels she was unpractised in walking in.

She tried to text the cab driver to let her know she was on her way but her fingers were all over the place.

All she had to do was get to the front entrance, get in her cab and get to her hotel. Three simple things easily achieved, or they would be if her feet and fingers would work properly.

In the morning she would fly back to London and complete the application form for the New York ballet company.

That was all she allowed herself to focus on. She would not think of the man she had just left behind.

An usher, who was shrugging a coat on, saw her approach and stepped in front of her. 'Is everything all right, miss?'

'Everything's fine. Why do you ask?'

The usher looked embarrassed. 'You're crying.'

'I am?' Putting a hand to her face, Chloe was horrified to find it wet with tears.

'Can I get you something? A coffee? Something stronger?'

'No, no, I need to get to my cab.' As she spoke her phone buzzed. It was the cab driver telling her she had five minutes to get to her or she would have to leave for her next job.

Panic now setting in, Chloe put a hand on the usher for support and leaned down to pull her heels off.

Shoes in one hand, phone clutched in the other, she set off at a run.

Had she thought the theatre's corridors wide when she'd arrived earlier? Now they seemed to have shrunk, the sides pressing closer and closer to her.

She picked up speed as she spotted the staircase, and kept close to the side as she ran down steps that seemed to go on and on, winding and winding, the exit so near and yet so far.

As soon as she reached the bottom she sprinted, running as fast as she had ever run in her life, the people she streamed past nothing but blurs.

Everything was a blur.

But still she ran until the warm night air hit her face and she was outside.

The cab driver, the same woman who had dropped her off hours before, tooted.

Doubling over as the first signs of a stitch set in, Chloe hobbled to the car, gasping for air.

Hand on the passenger door, she went to open it but then found her fingers still refusing to work.

The driver wound the window down and said something to her. It was nothing but noise to Chloe's ears, that distant sound of interference like a car radio going through a tunnel.

She spun around and stared up at the magnificent theatre, the name 'Compania de Ballet de Casillas' proudly embossed in gold leaf around the silhouette of a dancer in motion above the entrance door.

The Casillas Ballet Company. Named after the beloved mother of two boys whose life had been so cruelly taken at the hands of their father, her own husband.

A ballet company bought to keep her memory alive, a state-of-the-art theatre, dance school and facilities created from nothing to showcase the best that ballet had to offer, all to honour the memory of the woman they had loved.

Luis had loved his mother. Twenty-two years after her death and still he loved her. Javier had loved her too. For the first time in months she allowed a wave of tenderness into her heart for a man who had also lost so much, a man who'd clamped down on his feelings so tightly and effectively that he could deliberately cheat his oldest friend.

Luis hadn't clamped down on his feelings. Luis had opened his heart and embraced them—for her.

He had laid his heart on the line for the first time since his mother had died and Chloe, out of rabid fear, had turned it down.

She had dreamed of the day he declared his love for her then learned that dreams never came true.

But what if they did?

Luis *loved* her.

That was a truth.

He had seen all the good and bad in her just as she had seen the best and worst in him and still he loved her.

If she ran away now…

She would never have this chance again.

This was her time, *their* time, if only she had the courage to accept that sometimes dreams *did* come true, even for people like her and Luis whose own fathers could not bring themselves to love them.

Working automatically, she dug her hand into her clutch bag and pulled out the cash she had ready for the cab and thrust it into the driver's hand, unable to speak, able to apologise only with her eyes.

On legs that felt drugged, she walked back up the stairs and into the theatre foyer. The tears pouring down her face were so thick she struggled to see. She sensed the concerned faces surrounding her but blocked them all out.

Oh, Luis, where are you?

He couldn't still be in the costume room. Could he?

'Chloe?'

She spun round to the sound of the voice she knew so well and loved so much, and there he was, only feet away.

She didn't need her vision to see the haggard state of him.

How had she not seen it before?

'What's wrong?' Concern laced his every syllable. 'Have you been hurt?'

She shook her head, trying desperately to stop

the tears that were falling like a waterfall, trying desperately to speak through a throat that
had choked.

Her limbs took control of matters for her, legs
propelling her to him, arms throwing themselves
around him and holding him tightly, so tightly,
burying herself to him.

Only his innate strength stopped them buckling
under the weight of her ambush and after a moment where he fought to keep them steady and
upright, his strong arms wrapped around her as
tightly as she clung to him and his face buried
into her hair, his warm breath seeping through
to her skin.

'Oh, Luis,' she sobbed, 'I'm sorry. I'm sorry. I
love you so much it hurts. I'm sorry for hurting
you and for...'

But two large hands gently cupped her face to
tilt her head back. The dark hazel eyes she loved
so much were gazing down at her with a tenderness dreams were made of.

'My love,' he breathed. 'Please, say no more.
It is *I* who am sorry.'

She shook her head, fresh tears spilling free.
'I love you.'

'And I love you, with all my heart. I swear, I will never hurt you again. You are my life, Chloe, please believe that.'

'I do. Because it is the same for me. I don't want to live without you.'

'You won't,' he promised reverently. 'You and I will never be parted again.'

'Promise?'

'Promise.'

'For ever?'

'For ever.'

And then his lips found her and they kissed with such love and such passion that neither doubted the other's love again.

EPILOGUE

THE SUN SETTING over the Caribbean like an enormous jewel was a glorious sight and one Luis gazed at with full appreciation.

'How are the nerves holding up?'

He turned his head and smiled at Benjamin. 'No nerves.'

The Frenchman raised a brow that was a perfect imitation of his sister. 'No nerves?'

'None. This is a day I have been looking forward to for so long I think I might burst if she makes me wait any longer.' Chloe had insisted they not rush into exchanging their vows, reasoning that as they were only going to do it the once, she wanted it to be perfect for them.

Benjamin laughed. 'My sister can be very stubborn.'

'It's a family trait.'

'*Oui.*' A flash of white teeth. 'A trait I imagine will be inherited by my niece or nephew.'

'She told you?'

'She told Freya. Who told me…'

Luis burst into laughter.

Chloe had taken the pregnancy test only the week before and had made him swear not to tell anyone until the first trimester had passed.

He should have guessed she wouldn't be able to contain herself from telling Freya.

After the first heady days when they had finally declared their love for each other, days spent in bed, surfacing only for food, all forms of contraception forgotten about, Luis had come out of the daze determined to make things right with Benjamin.

Chloe had elicited her sister-in-law's help in the matter, Freya falling under her spell enough to forgive Chloe's part in Benjamin's kidnapping of her. With his wife and sister both on his case over the matter, Benjamin had eventually given in and accepted a meeting with him, just the two men, in a neutral venue.

Naturally, that had meant Chloe and Freya had come along to the chosen hotel too, doing a terrible job of hiding behind menus at a table on the other side of the room.

Luis knew it was their presence there that had given Benjamin the impetus to hear him out. He'd refused Luis's cheque that equalled the total profit lost, plus interest, telling him to donate it to charity. But he had accepted a beer from him. And he had listened.

Three beers each later and Benjamin had apologised for his own terrible deeds.

Five beers each later and they were cracking jokes together.

And now, two months on, Benjamin was to be Luis's best man as he married the woman who had stolen his heart then given it back to him whole with her own nestled in with it.

The only fly in the ointment was Javier's absence.

His twin had cut himself off so effectively a French guillotine could not have severed it better.

Chloe kept telling him to give Javier time but Luis knew his brother better than anyone.

For Javier it was simple. By choosing Chloe, Luis had switched his loyalty. His brother could not accept or understand that it hadn't been a choice for Luis; his love for Chloe was all encompassing, his need to be with her as necessary as breathing.

But then he forgot all about his estranged twin for the woman he loved appeared on deck, radiant in a floor-length lace white wedding dress that showed off her mountainous breasts—*Dios*, early pregnancy really suited her—and holding a posy of flowers over her non-existent bump. Her smile illuminated everyone. Even Captain Brand, officiating at the wedding, smiled broadly along with the rest of the crew.

Chloe made no attempt to walk serenely to him, bounding over like the galloping gazelle who had thrown her arms around him all those months ago.

The beaming smile didn't leave her face for a moment as they exchanged their vows. When the time came for them to share their first kiss as husband and wife she threw her arms around him and kissed him for so long they missed the first set of fireworks.

With his beautiful wife snuggled securely in his arms, Luis watched the spectacular display and reflected that he was the luckiest man to have sailed these waters.

* * *

Luis and Chloe Casillas are delighted to announce the birth of their first child, Clara Louise Casillas, born at 5.22 a.m., weighing 7lb 3oz. Both mother and daughter are doing well.

* * * * *